ROYALLY FAKE FIANCÉ

LEE SAVINO

FREE BOOK!

Grab it here! https://BookHip.com/ZPKRZL

ROYALLY FAKE FIANCÉ

It's the age old love story: Girl meets Duke. Girl hates Duke. Duke proposes marriage.

The only thing I hate worse than stuck up rich guys are ones with royal titles. But the Duke of New Arcadia has an image problem only a fiancée can fix, and I'm the only woman who can play the part.

For college tuition and permanent citizenship, I'll pretend to be his Cinderella. I can handle royal makeovers, fancy balls, persistent paparazzi, and suspicious family members.

But then our fake attraction turns real. Forget glass slippers, this Cinderella is in danger of losing her heart.

Royally Fake Fiancé is a stand alone royal romance starring one arrogant Duke and the klutzy commoner who steals his heart. Witty banter, slow burn shenanigans, explosive private moments (literally, things explode) — the royal house of New Arcadia will never be the same again!

CHAPTER 1

rankie

"OH YEAH, baby. That's the spot. That's the spot."

Not again. I swivel in my chair and give the kitchen wall the evil eye.

"Give it to me, big boy. Oh yeah. Oh yeah."

The espresso maker gurgles and shoots a stream of frothed milk into my mug. I slide off the chair and walk around the bar to collect it.

The shrieking continues a few rooms over, faint but clear. "Oh yeah. Oh yeah. Oh yeah."

I detour and slam my hand against a patch of bare wall between two oil paintings of lemons. "Will you stop?"

Silence. I check the paintings to make sure my thumping on the wall didn't disturb them and head back to the new love of my life, the object of my desire, the fresh steaming liquid from heaven that is my morning latte.

I'm about to take a sip when the voice calls again, "Give it to me, big boy."

"Enough!" I set down my cup with all the reverence of the Archbishop of Canterbury lowering a crown. Then I stride out of the palatial kitchen, my splurge purchase silk robe billowing out behind me like a cape. "I don't think so. Not again."

I round the corner and almost take out a giant vase. With a growl, I gather my robe close and ease sideways between two Louis XVI armchairs. I keep forgetting this place is a museum. It's a miracle I haven't taken out a Ming vase by now.

"Give it to me. Give it to me. Oh yeah. Oh yeah!"

Another corner, and I narrowly miss getting impaled on a lance. I stop long enough to carefully retract the gauntlet and its ancient weapon, glaring at the suit of armor as I maneuver its arm into its regular, upright position. "Bum arm, Sir Fred? Carpal tunnel?"

The suit of armor doesn't answer.

I hustle past Sir Fred—gingerly—and speed through the outer hall, past more oil paintings full of naked folk frolicking through epic landscapes. The naked frolics are all the more creepy with the porn-like commentary.

"Oh yeah! That's the spot!"

The closer I get to the voice, the smaller and more crackly it sounds, like it's coming from a hidden radio. I open a door and humidity blasts me in the face. Sunlight shines full bore from a skylight onto a thick canopy of leaves. The room before me is a jungle. A literal jungle. Or as close to one as a sunroom full of jungle plants can be.

The voice falters a moment, then continues full force: "That's the spot! Oh yeah!"

"Oh no," I shout. "I've waited. I've been patient. You have been at it… All. Night. Long!" I step over the threshold to the grand sunroom, batting giant banana leaves out of my way. My robe brushes fountaining ferns that have been growing since the Jurassic era. I bushwhack gently towards the hot'n'heavy commentary, wishing I'd brought a machete.

Not for the plants. For the loud-mouthed 'lover' who has crowed for the last time.

"Big boy! Big boy!" The sound of wings fluttering makes me change course. I duck under a flowering branch and head to the front of the room where giant windows overlook a manicured garden.

A parrot, grey except for white patches around his eyes and a splash of red on his tail, sits on his perch in a patch of light, bobbing his head in time to his cries. "Yes! Yes! Yes!"

I clear my throat.

The sound cuts off abruptly. The bird twitches, cocking his head at me.

I fold my arms across my chest. "Are you finished?"

"Big boy?" the bird gurgles.

"No." I raise a finger. "I've had enough. I was okay with this… the first time. Even the second and third times. I thought it was funny. Now you know what I'm thinking? No? I'll tell you." I level my finger at the bird. "Parrot à la King!"

I stalk forward, my finger still out. The bird dances from foot to foot as I approach, nervously fluffing his feathers.

"Roasted parrot," I enunciate clearly. "Kung pao parrot. Parrot cacciatore."

The parrot ducks his head as if in contrition. I'm not fooled. There is nothing but mischief in his beady little eyes.

His curved beak seems to grin as it asks again, "Big boy?"

"Parrot tikka masala!" I reach the perch. Ignoring my threats, the parrot scoots closer and cranes his head under my outstretched finger, begging me to scratch his neck. With a sigh, I oblige.

After a few seconds, the parrot lets out a crackly, "Oh yeah."

"You just can't help yourself," I mutter, massaging the grey parrot's feathered neck until bits of white fluff waft around us.

Instead of answering, the parrot angles his head in the opposite direction, pushing on my hand when I hesitate to keep scratching.

"Enough with the commentary while I'm drinking my coffee. I don't know what idiot let you watch porn." Actually, I do. It was probably the parrot's owner, who by my guess is a little old lady. Never married, no children, and overly endowed in the bank account, with a passion for French revival furniture and garden topiaries. Oh, and for Elvis. The pompadour-haired singer, and the parrot she named after him.

"Are you going to be good?" I ask Elvis, who is practically crooning in pleasure as I scratch his scrawny neck.

"Oh yeah." The parrot ruffles his feathers, sending out a fresh wave of dander to float in the sun. I back away, grab a hand vacuum, and clean up a little. At least the bird poops in one place. Either that, or the army of professional house cleaners that comes in once a week spends most of their time in here, washing and buffing the glossy leaves of the banana tree plants.

"Fine. I'll play you some music." A few feet away from the perch is a sleek console containing a vintage record player and records in sleeves. The room is rigged with state of the art speakers. No expense spared for Elvis the bird.

"All shook up, all shook up," the parrot whistles as I load a record. "Give it to me, big boy."

I leave him bobbing his head in time to 'Blue Suede Shoes' and hope the neighbors have sound proofed their own breakfast nook. At this rate, Elvis will be singing all day, with angry porn-tastic narrative in between whenever the record turns over.

By the time I've traversed the mile back to the kitchen, my latte is cold. I drink it anyway.

I knew this pet sitting job would be different from my usual, but this is another dimension. Lately, most of my clients have been well off, wealthy enough to hire someone to care for their pet while they're traveling for months at a time.

But there's wealth and then there's *wealth.* The fact was impressed upon me when I went to rap on the door to Elvis's home, and the door opened before I could touch it. I promptly overbalanced and fell over, right at the butler's feet. A *butler.* In this day and age! I gaped at him from the polished floor. He looked at me like I was a bit of muck stuck to his shiny shoe.

That's when I knew I wasn't being hired to watch a parrot for a year. I was being paid to nanny a bird the owner loved more than a child. A child you left at home with a nanny while you traveled the world for a year, but apparently, rich people do that.

Elvis came with a ninety-five page handwritten manual, which is one page shorter than the manual issued with the space-age espresso maker built into the kitchen wall. But the job comes with a free stay in a nine thousand square foot mansion. No gardening or house-cleaning required—the owner has separate staff who visit for that.

And she's gone for a 'grand tour' which includes several continents, and traveling by planes, trains, and automobiles. And boats. Can't forget the boats. Or yachts, as rich people call them.

Luckily, the butler isn't around to look down his nose at me. Once he'd let me in and given me a tour, he left to catch up with his employer. Lady Drey is paying him and a maid to travel *with her*.

Leaving me and her espresso machine to live happily ever after. Or, at least, for the next ten months.

I finish a second latte—I deserve it—and stretch. My agenda for the day: coffee, check on Elvis, take a long bath, check on Elvis, watch an old movie in the theater room. Maybe I'll let Elvis watch with me. He loves Cary Grant.

My room is in the east wing, near to Elvis' jungle room. But it's no servant's quarters. I have a private bathroom, and a walk-in closet bigger than the bedroom at my old apartment. The bathroom has a bathtub in the corner, with windows overlooking the garden and the Tudor style mansion next door. A *lot* of windows. More windows than anyone should be comfortable with in a bathroom, but okay… I shrug off my robe, exhibitionist style, and fill the bath, adding a generous amount of bubble wash. I don't bother with modesty—even if someone wanted to spy through the second story windows, I've never seen anyone next door. Once in a while there's a car in the drive, but they probably avoid the side of their house closest to Elvis. Even from here, I can still hear faint strains of 'Blue Suede Shoes', along with the occasional shriek from the parrot.

I sink into the luxuriously hot water and frothy bubbles, and prop my feet up.

"A bath at ten in the morning. So leisurely." I do my best Katherine Hepburn impression. One must always talk like Katherine Hepburn when one stays in a mansion.

I never thought I'd ever live like a rich person. My parents were barely working class. I thought I'd be more uncomfortable living in a mansion, but I quickly got used to it.

Maybe I can add mansion-sitting to my resume. Find another lady on grand tour, with a house full of antiques and a garden full of topiaries, and a parrot perched… in a tree?

"Elvis," I gasp, jolting up in the bath. I lose my balance and fall back. A tsunami of soapy water hits me in the face.

"Shit!" I sputter and haul myself out, my feet threatening to slide on the soaked marble floor. I grab my robe and pelt downstairs, wet hair flying. I pause before the door to the garden, my robe twisted around my wet body, and spot Elvis perched on a Japanese maple.

"How did you get out?" I cry, and throw open the door. My exit startles the bird, who flaps away, over the low stone wall dividing Lady's Drey's property from her neighbor's. Ducking low, in my own version of stealth mode, I scramble over the wall and sneak through boxwoods and rhododendrons, clutching my robe tight to keep the silk from snagging on the manicured branches.

The grey parrot lands above me, on the rail of the neighbor's sprawling deck.

"Elvis," I hiss.

The parrot cocks his head at me, not impressed. I need to trap him, but all I have is my robe. I tug it off and sneak around to the deck stairs, where I pause to say a prayer to St. Francis, patron saint of animals. Surely he's also the patron saint of pet sitters.

Elvis glides down to the deck, four feet in front of me.

Thank you, I mouth, and stalk forward, bare-assed, robe outstretched between two hands. I'm just about to snag the escapee bird when the deck door glides open. A tall, dark-haired man steps through, mug in hand, undoubtedly about to enjoy his coffee while looking over his garden on this fine, quiet morning.

A quiet morning that is ruined by Elvis, the African Grey parrot, zooming past his head and me, wide-eyed and completely nude, streaking after it, screaming, "Don't let him out!"

* * *

Two hours earlier...

Benedict

THE WOMAN across from me doesn't look happy. "Benedict, I'm pregnant."

"Congratulations," I say solemnly, matching her serious tone.

"Indeed." The queen's mouth sets in a hard line. Not quite a frown.

She couldn't have picked a better place to deliver the news. Palaces are such gloomy places. Their exteriors are so grand on TV, so beautiful and luminous, with guards and gates surrounding them to keep out the commoners. But inside is palatial and dark, with that particular smell I associate with antique furniture. No matter how often the place is cleaned, no matter how spic and span the huge expanses of parquet floors and thick carpets are kept, the air feels heavy and old, pregnant with the weight of centuries and countless decisions made by my ancestors. Every conversation gains gravitas. The fate of nations rests in each word.

If I ever become king, I will not enjoy moving into the palace. But I will do it. It would be my duty.

"How are you feeling?" I ask the queen. She looks paler than normal. Morning sickness?

"Fine," she sighs and flicks her hand. "Much to my doctors' surprise."

"Yes, well..." I shift in my chair, searching for a way to approach the subject delicately.

"Just say it." The queen raises her chin. She didn't miss how closely I was studying her. "I'm too old. Everybody knows it."

"Forty-five is hardly ancient," I protest and she snorts.

"I may as well be. Pregnant. After all these years?" She shakes her head with mild disapproval, as if her pregnancy is an unruly diplomat who's arrived ten minutes late to an audience, unforgivably tardy.

She leans forward and pushes a red folder across the low table towards me. "It's a high risk pregnancy, of course. My age is enough to make it so. But also..." She nods to the folder and I open it to see for myself.

A large, black and white ultrasound shot greets me. I flip past it to a page of three smaller ultrasound pictures, labeled 'Baby 1', '2', and '3'.

"Triplets," I breathe.

"Indeed." The queen rises and when I rise with her, she waves me down. She paces to the giant floor-to-ceiling windows framed with waterfalls of royal blue curtains. "I'll be lucky if I'm not put on bedrest before the month is out. The press release is scheduled for the Midsummer Ball."

I calculate the time in my head. "That's a week away."

"Yes. And a week from then, I will name my official heir."

I shift my weight in the chair and it creaks. I abandon all attempts to sit comfortably. "Why now?"

"You know why," she says impatiently. For a moment, she is not the queen. She is my aunt, quizzing me after my lessons.

Of course I know why. She is forty-five, and pregnant for the first time, with triplets. As healthy as she is, with the best medical care in the world, it's still considered a high risk pregnancy. As soon as the news breaks, the whole country will be wondering whether their queen will survive.

"I know why," I say. "But you haven't officially secured succession all these years. To do so now would be—"

"A vote of no confidence?" Her voice is drier than the Sahara. "In the face of my own mortality, it doesn't matter. We are Lyonnesse. We do our duty."

I straighten. She's right. The Lyonnesse line has done their duty, ruling for five hundred years.

The window's light halos her as she turns to face me. "If something happens to me before…" she takes a deep breath, "before the birth, the country will need a steady hand. As the eldest son of my deceased sister, you stand in line for the throne."

I tilt my chin. I am aware. We've had many conversations to this effect, in this very room.

"I have not formally acknowledged you as heir, for reasons you know. The public has accepted this, but in light of the news of my pregnancy, they will expect a formal announcement. And I will make it. A week after Midsummer."

I swallow. "I would be honored to serve—"

"It will be either you, or your brother."

I sag back in the chair like I've been struck. "My brother?" My usual reserve is gone as I reel from the shock.

"Indeed." The queen is watching me with something like pity in her brown eyes.

"But why?" I've been groomed for this moment since my mother died. I've gone to the best schools, gotten the best grades, worked the best internships. I endured years of thankless work, interning at each Ministry before accepting my dream job at the Ministry of Finance. There isn't a junior government official who doesn't know me by sight, if not by name, and not because I appear regularly in the tabloids. I do not.

Unlike my brother.

"My career and service have been exemplary." Understatement. I didn't just accept success as my due, I worked for it. I never partied, never caused a scandal, never stepped one toe out of line. I've been perfect.

"I know. If it were entirely up to me…" My aunt doesn't shrug—queens don't shrug—but her jaw tightens as if she's holding back what she really wants to say.

"Isn't it? Up to you?"

The queen doesn't answer my question. I knew my enemies wanted to get their hooks into her, but I had no idea they had succeeded. "Benedict, there's a very high chance it will be you. But you can't afford any mistakes. Not now. Not with everyone watching."

"But Franz—"

"Your brother is wild, to be sure."

"Wild?" Another understatement. "He organized a regatta down the Regin river, on the night of your Silver Jubilee. All his crew friends in their fathers' yachts."

The queen closes her eyes, her lips pressed together. "I remember."

"It caught fire. And that wasn't even one of his more destructive parties."

"He's straightened up since then. His military superiors report he's taken to discipline."

"And every time he goes on leave, he ends up in the tabloids." I snort.

"You know how they are."

They being the press. The paparazzi. Hungry, vicious sharks. "Yes, I do. And I may have a certain strike against me, but Franz is a complete wastrel."

"The strike in question, dear nephew, isn't a small matter. If it got out, it would be the scandal that would eclipse all other scandals." The queen settles into a chair closer to me.

In a rare gesture, she covers my hand with hers. "We've worked hard to come to this day."

"I am ready to serve."

"I know. And I will do everything in my power to be sure it will be you."

"Is there anything I can do?" I haven't done everything perfectly, only to have it all snatched away now.

My aunt purses her lips. This is what she's been unhappy about. "Yes. There is one matter." She nods to the second folder on the table before her.

I lean in and take it, opening it to reveal half-blurred photos. Not ultrasounds, not this time. These pictures are of me and a woman.

A naked woman.

Few details are clear—the photo was taken from far away, from a building opposite the hotel room. But one shot perfectly captures my face, and the fact that I'm holding a brunette. She's naked and pressed against me.

"The press forwarded these to my office before dawn. I called you here early to warn you."

I suck in a breath. "I can explain—"

The queen waves a hand. "I know you abhor the limelight. As much as your mother thrived in it. I, too, have shunned it. It is what a good ruler does."

My stomach is roiling, but I maintain a level tone. "Can you stop these photos from running?"

"It's too late. The first printing is already done. I'm sure it's hit the streets by now." The queen shudders delicately. "I can only imagine what they're speculating. And Benedict," she gives me her gimlet stare, "we can't afford for them to speculate."

"I know," I murmur. "I know." Everything I've worked for. Everything I've fought to rise above. One instance, one accident of fate, and it's all ruined. Everything.

I realize I'm gripping the edge of one photo too hard, and force my fingers to straighten. I place the pictures back in the folder, refusing to crumple them like I want to. "I'll fix it."

The queen's shoulders relax the slightest bit. She's worried. The pregnancy, the threat of scandal, crowning a new leader the people can trust—each is an added layer of stress. I can't do anything about the first, but I can shoulder the rest.

"I'll fix it," I repeat. A Lyonnesse does his duty.

The queen gives a regal nod. "See that you do."

* * *

"It was an accident," I tell Daniel, head of my PR team, as I stride out of the palace with my phone pressed to my ear.

"Of course it was. The Duke of New Arcadia, caught with a lady of the night? It's not your MO."

I duck into my waiting car and direct my driver to take me home. Then I roll up the privacy window so I can speak freely.

"She wasn't a lady of the night." I grit my teeth before I admit the next part. "She was Wyndam Bennett."

"Winnie Bennett?" Daniel chokes. "Heir to the Bennett Hotel chain? Reality TV star and B movie actress?"

I force my jaw to unclench. "The same. I didn't know she was in a movie."

A snort. "She's the lead in at least two leaked sex tapes. I've seen one. I'd rate it a B." Daniel sounds thoughtful, but he often uses a smooth, soothing tone to deliver sarcasm. "Isn't she in rehab?"

"She was. She left. She's back now."

"Why am I only now hearing about this?" Daniel demands.

"I handled it."

"Clearly." More sarcasm. I can hear papers flipping as he looks through printouts of the paparazzi pictures I forwarded to him.

"She was drunk, or on something," I say. "Probably both. It was an accident. She saw me enter my hotel room, and stumbled in after me. The camera person must have been watching through the window." I grimace. "Trying to catch me at something."

"And it paid off. For once."

"Quite." My tone is cold enough to freeze a finger off. "Daniel, I can't afford for them to go digging."

Daniel knows my secret. As head of PR, his main job is to keep it buried. "We need to control the narrative," he says.

"We could tell the truth."

"That's the last thing we want to do. The Crown Prince of New Arcadia, shacking up with the country's top tabloid darling? While she was drunk and/or strung out?"

"We weren't shacking up."

"Says you. What will Winnie Bennett say?"

I groan.

"Exactly," Daniel says. "We can't ask. She'll spin it the way she wants it. And she wants to be the reigning star of Page Six. Dating you would get her everything she wants."

I groan again.

"You're lucky her face isn't in these pictures. Does anyone else know it was her?"

"I don't think so." I try to remember the details of that nightmarish night. "I bundled her back to her room as quickly as I could. I used her phone to call her father, who sent a car. The next day, he called my private line to thank me for my discretion and tell me Winnie had been checked back into rehab."

"Where she will hopefully stay for the next two weeks. Excellent. With your permission, I'll call Daddy Bennett and make sure the family stays quiet. And then it'll be up to us to spin the story." I can hear Daniel rubbing his hands together. Sometimes I wonder if he would prefer me to lead a more interesting social life. If that's the case, he'd be better off managing PR for Franz, my younger brother.

"And how, pray tell, do we spin this?" I ask.

"I should think it would be obvious."

"Is it?" I pinch the bridge of my nose.

"Of course." Daniel's breezy tone tells me I'm not going to like his solution. "You find a woman who looks exactly like Winnie Bennett, and marry her."

* * *

My head is still ringing with Daniel's advice when I reach home. *Find a woman who looks exactly like Winnie Bennett, and marry her.* Before Midsummer.

I can only imagine the casting call. *Leggy brunette wanted. Body type to match nude photos already dispersed by the press. Must be willing to sign an extensive pre-nup.*

"It'll work perfectly," Daniel insisted. "At least we don't have to match a certain shoe size." He laughed at his own quip.

I ended the call to keep from shouting at him.

My driver deposits me on my front stoop. My home is modest-sized—barely ten thousand square feet. Classic architecture with the interiors decorated in a modern style, just the way I like it. I head to my kitchen, make my usual breakfast smoothie on autopilot, and pour it into a mug so I can carry it outside.

Find a woman who looks exactly like Winnie Bennett, and marry her.

Daniel is brilliant at PR—most of the time—but there is no way this sort of elaborate farce will work. I'm better off declaring a one night stand with Winnie Bennett, complete with garish sex toys and a drug buffet.

It's a glorious summer day. Perfect weather for me to stare into my garden and contemplate my fate. Birdsong greets me as I slide open the door and step onto my deck.

I'm about to take a sip of my smoothie when a grey blur whizzes by my head. Before I can react, a sultry-eyed woman rises from my deck stairs like a dark-haired version of 'The Birth of Venus' by Botticelli.

Like Botticelli's Venus, she is naked. Utterly and completely *naked*.

Unlike Botticelli's Venus, she is not serenely rising from the ocean. She flies across my deck, shrieking, "Don't let him out!" and runs straight past me… into my home.

enedict

FOR A MOMENT I STAND, blinking at my backyard. Then I pivot and follow the banshee. The brunette is completely naked, and waving a white flag over her head. Not a flag, actually, some sort of garment—a bathrobe. My impromptu guest dashes to and fro, using the robe to try to catch the parrot.

I should help her, but I can only stare. The woman is pale and curvy, of middling height. If she would stand still a moment, her head would barely come up to my chin.

Her damp hair flies around her face, strands catching on her flushed cheeks, but doing nothing to obscure her body. Her breasts bounce as she races around the room. Beautiful, bountiful breasts, perfect enough to give Botticelli heart palpitations and make him reach for his paints.

She looks vaguely familiar.

Mid-chase, my brunette Venus screeches to a halt and whirls on me.

"Shut the door!" she screams, waving wildly at the exit to my porch.

Mutely, I obey.

I need to get hold of myself. I have a wild woman chasing a parrot around my home. I should help catch the bird, and then find out what exactly is going on.

I have several questions. Is she my neighbor? An exotic bird breeder? An ornithologist? My dick would like to know if she's a full or part time nudist.

First, I have to catch the parrot.

"Finally," the siren says when I stalk to her side. "Took you long enough. A little help here?"

"What's the plan?" I need to stay focused on the grey bird because if I look down at her, I'm going to get distracted. The parrot has flapped to a grand piano and alighted on my bust of Chopin. As I watch, it cocks its tail and defecates.

"I was going to try to trap him in my robe." She gnaws her lip, totally focused on her quarry. If she realizes she's naked, it makes not a whit of difference to her.

"Allow me." I grab a cream-colored throw off my couch and advance, moving as stealthily as I can in a suit.

"Don't kill it," she hisses.

"I won't," I mutter. I'm almost to the piano. "Polly want a cracker?" I say under my breath.

The parrot cocks its head to the side; fixes one beady black eye on me. "Give it to me, big boy," it croaks, and launches himself off the bust, directly at me.

* * *

Frankie

. . .

THE MAN whose home I've invaded stalks forward, blanket stretched between his elegant hands. He's a tall drink of water, lean and fit in a way that tells me he's got muscles under his suit. His elegant, three-piece suit is perfectly fitted in every way, right down to his polished shoes, and crisp pocket hanky made of lavender silk. He's a poster boy for a GQ article: *Top 10 Reasons to Wear a Three Piece Suit Always*, even when relaxing on your back porch at ten in the morning.

Mr. Suit has pale skin and a close-cropped black beard that highlights the fantastic structure of his face. I'm not usually into facial hair, but in his case, I'm making an exception.

Of course, I'd find anyone attractive if they'll help me capture this damn bird. And it looks like he's going to nab Elvis. He's half crouched in a way that stretches his slacks over his perfectly shaped derriere. Not that I'm staring.

"That's it," I whisper. Mr. Suit is about to grab Elvis when the bird parrots his favorite line, flaps off his perch, and flies into the man's face.

Even if you're a bird lover, an explosion of grey feathers in your face trips the evolutionary 'Fight or Flight' switch. Mr. Suit jerks backwards, his arms flying up to shield himself. Halfway into his Flight mode, Mr. Suit's reflexes switch to Fight. He ducks the attacking bird, regains his balance, and whirls to toss the blanket in the parrot's direction.

"Elvis!" I cry, rushing forward to keep my bird from getting hurt. I trip on the carpet and pitch forward just as Mr. Suit turns. We crash into each other. He tries to catch me, but my forward motion, combined with his lack of balance, causes us to tip over, me in Mr. Suit's arms. We land on the ground together, a tangle of limbs.

The heavy sound of fluttering wings tells me Elvis has gotten away safely.

Thank you, St. Francis. I gasp in Mr. Suit's arms, trying to catch my breath as a lone grey feather floats down on top of us.

I rise up enough to swat Mr. Suit on the shoulder. "What the hell was that? Were you trying to kill him?"

"I beg your pardon?" Mr. Suit says. It sounds very polite in his crisp, upper crust accent, but he's glaring at me. Well, not directly at me. His face is carefully averted, his gaze fixed across the room. His body is stiff underneath me.

Really, really stiff.

That's when I remember: *I'm naked.*

"Oh shit," I say and start to scramble off him.

"Indeed," he mutters and tries to rise also. We both over-balance and fall together. This time, he lands half on top of me. I try to move, and my legs tangle with his impossibly long ones. He's bigger up close. Heavier too. Well equipped to win this impromptu wrestling match, but I'm determined.

"Get off me," I shout, pushing at him.

"I beg your pardon, madam. I am trying to," he says in that infuriatingly posh tone. My unbred ears detect a subtle layer of accusation, but he's too polite to do more than insin-uate that I'm the clumsy cause of all this.

"Do you always talk like you have a stick up your ass?"

Mr. Suit's black brows jerk together. "I beg your pardon?" The look he gives me could scorch off all my hair.

"Yes, exactly, like that," I grumble.

"I could ask you a similar question," he says, his voice dripping acid.

"Whatever." I shove his shoulder, and he rolls to his back. I fight my way up, but I have insufficient leverage, and topple back onto his firm chest just as a second pair of polished shoes crosses the parquet floor.

"Well now, this is unexpected," says a coolly amused voice.

I rear back but before I can roll away, Mr. Suit says, "Daniel," and heaves upwards, pulling me with him. I grab his shirt to keep from falling over again.

Daniel is another tall, lean man in a suit, with dark skin and a smoothly shaved bald head. He sets down a slim, black briefcase, and appraises Mr. Suit and me with satisfaction.

"It's not what it looks like," Mr. Suit barks, and jerks out of his suit jacket. Only when he pulls it around my shoulders do I realize the situation. I am standing, *naked,* in another man's home. In the circle of his arms.

Once the jacket is in place, I release Mr. Suit's shirt like it burned my palms, and back away.

"Isn't it, though?" Daniel saunters forward. "It looks like you found her. Well done, Your Grace."

"Found who?" I clutch the suit jacket around me tighter.

"She's not—" Mr. Suit begins, and then his dark brows snap together as he fixes me with an intense stare.

"What?" I ask, trying to hide the way my belly flips in his presence. "I'm not what?"

"Unbelievable," Mr. Suit breathes.

"She's perfect." Daniel circles me. "A little heavier than Winnie, but we can work with that."

"Heavier?" I echo.

"We can work with that," Daniel assures me, and swivels to Mr. Suit. "Did you ask her?"

"Ask me what?" I look back and forth. Both men are taller than me, so I feel like a child with her parents talking over her head. *Talking about me.*

"No," says Mr. Suit, ignoring me. "I need to explain."

"Explain what?" I snap.

"She might say yes… you never know until you ask."

I flinch when Daniel reaches out and brushes my hair

back from my face. "Hey!" I back away in outrage. Elvis chooses this moment to fly to my shoulder.

"Oh, hello." Daniel remains unfazed at the appearance of a parrot. "And who is this?"

"Give it to me, big boy," Elvis chirps. "That's the spot."

"Oh my." Daniel draws back, his elegant hand fluttering to his chest. "Darling, buy me dinner first." He switches his attention to me. "Is it always so forward?"

"Yes. He's a parrot."

"What sort of parrot?"

"An African Grey," I answer automatically. "They're big talkers."

"Yours?" Daniel cocks his head, and Elvis copies the movement.

This is ridiculous. "No. I'm parrot-sitting over there." I jab a finger in the direction of the house next door, readjusting so I can hold the suit jacket. My jerky movements make Elvis squawk and fluff his wings. "I don't know how he got out, but I'll make sure it doesn't happen again—"

"Wait." Daniel's shaved head swivels between me and Mr. Suit. "This was all an accident?"

"Yes." I edge backwards. I don't entirely know what's going on with these two exquisitely dressed men, but I am naked and messy and distinctly out of place. "It won't happen again."

"I've never seen her before she ran inside, chasing the bird," Mr. Suit adds. I shoot him a glare for throwing me under the bus. He parries with one eloquent, raised eyebrow.

"My goodness," Daniel says. "Now that's what I call Fate. You see the resemblance, of course," he asks Mr. Suit, who dips his chin, never taking his eyes off me.

"What resemblance?" I should go, but my feet are cemented to the floor. Mr. Suit is looking at me like no one ever has. Under his suit jacket, my skin flushes.

"It's uncanny. If I may, darling." Daniel puts a finger under my chin and tips my face to the side. I'm so surprised, I let him. "Similar features, slightly different bone structure, but if you'll notice her profile—"

"Okay." I step out of reach. "That's enough of that. And don't call me 'darling.'"

Daniel backs away, palms up, but he's smiling. "What's your name?"

"Frankie. And this is Elvis." I glance towards the back door.

"Enchanté," Daniel says. "I'm Daniel. You'll forgive my forwardness. I am simply taken aback."

"Why?" I push my tangled mass of hair back, making Elvis extend his wings for balance.

"Because you're perfect. You, my dear, are exactly who we're looking for."

"For what?" I glower at both of them.

"Nothing nefarious. My goodness." Daniel chuckles. "No need to give us the evil eye. What happens in a duke's house stays in a duke's house."

"What?" *A duke?*

"Why yes. Didn't you know? You're in a duke's home."

"What, this place?" I say before I can stop myself. "This can't be a duke's home."

Daniel and Mr. Suit exchange glances.

"And why, pray tell, not?" Mr. Suit asks with enough condescension to make me grind my teeth "Are you an expert on dukes?"

"No. I'm American. It's just..." I shrug. "Seems kind of a dump."

Daniel sputters and turns his head, becoming very interested in inspecting his own briefcase. I suspect he is laughing. Mr. Suit stares at me like I'm a strange sort of bug he's never seen before.

"I mean, for a duke," I amend. "Don't they all live in castles?"

"No," Mr. Suit says with an entire lab's worth of acid in his tone. "As a matter of fact, we don't."

Aw, snap.

I gulp. "Um, I take it back. It's not a dump, it's a very nice home. Is it yours?"

"As a matter of fact, it is mine," Mr. Suit says.

"I thought a duke would live in a palace or a castle or something…" My babbling stops when my brain catches up. "Oh. If this is a duke's home, and you live here, then…"

Daniel turns back. "Allow me to introduce His Grace, the Duke of New Arcadia." Daniel keeps talking but I don't hear the rest. There's a blank space where my brain used to be. My thoughts are whited-out. I knew there was royalty here, in New Arcadia. They have a queen and everything. My own employer is called Lady Drey. But it's different meeting someone close to my age, with beautiful features and a GQ presence. He's someone I'd perv on.

He's someone I *am* perving on.

Shit! I am perving on a duke! In his home! Where I barged my way in, naked, chasing a parrot.

Daniel is still talking. He's facing the duke and leaning close, as if he's trying to convince His Grace of something. But the duke is still staring at me in a way that makes me hot and cold all over.

I cross my arms over my chest. Elvis chirps in my ear and squats slightly. A second later, a white-grey bead of parrot poop rolls down the bespoke suit sleeve.

"Oh, Elvis," I groan.

Daniel stops talking. Now they're both staring.

This is horrific. This is worse than the time I was in a beauty pageant and accidentally stepped on Donna Draper's dress and tore the bottom half clean off.

I'd say a prayer to St. Francis—*Please let me get out of here without dying of embarrassment*—but I don't think this situation is under his jurisdiction.

"Look, I didn't mean to intrude," I say to the duke. "Thanks for helping. And for the suit jacket. I'll clean it." I back away. I'm going to get Elvis back to Lady Drey's mansion, and then I'm going to clip his wings. It's either that, or choke him. "Can we just forget all this happened?"

"Wait," the duke says in his deep voice. "If you leave like this, he'll fly away."

I stop in my tracks. "Right." I consider stuffing the bird under the jacket, but I don't want to ruin it more—the suit jacket, not the bird.

"Does he have a cage?" the Duke of New Arcadia asks patiently.

"Yes."

"I'll go get it," Daniel says.

"No, that's okay—"

"I can go, and you two can talk." He emphasizes the word *talk*, and gives the duke a meaningful glance.

"Am I in trouble?" Shit, I didn't break any laws trespassing into a duke's house, did I? I don't want to be deported.

"Oh, no, no trouble. You might even say you're an answer to a prayer." Daniel winks at me.

At the gleam in his eye, I take a step back, and trip on a dining room chair. Elvis protests as I nearly fall over.

"Sit down, Frankie," the duke orders.

I sit so fast, Elvis spreads his wings for balance. Something in that ducal tone, so used to issuing orders, makes my body want to obey.

The duke continues, "Daniel, do you mind?"

"Not at all. Where is the cage, Frankie?"

"Um, in the Florida room… at least, that's what we call it in the States."

"The conservatory. Understood." Daniel arches a brow at me. "And while I am retrieving things, shall I find something for you to wear?"

"Oh, no, it's fine. I can just wear my robe."

"I'll just be a jiff!" Daniel slips through the door, leaving me alone, with a duke. I sit up straighter and cross my legs. I can almost hear my grandmother scolding me and my cousins to 'act like ladies.' *Too late, Grandmère.* She would have kittens—several litters—if she could see me now.

"Would you like something to drink?" the duke asks.

"Uh, no. No, thank you."

"Are you quite sure? I have tea, fruit juice… the remnants of a green smoothie." He crosses the kitchen and frowns into his mug.

"Oh no, I wouldn't drink that," I blurt. "I think Elvis pooped in it. Sorry…"

"No harm done." The duke sets the mug down. He returns to his seat and folds his long body into it. His hand extends across the table but he doesn't tap his fingers. He's perfectly still. He might as well be carved in marble. "How long have you been living next door?" he starts, just as I say,

"Are you going to deport me?"

The duke raises a dark brow. "No. Why would I? Have you done anything illegal?"

"No. But Daniel said something about 'you found her'. What did he mean?"

"Daniel is the head of my PR. He has… an interesting idea about how to fix a current scandal." The duke checks his watch.

"A scandal? Involving you?"

"Yes. Me and a woman of your description."

"Ah. And he thinks I can help?"

"Yes." The duke's eyes flick to me. Up and down and away. "I am skeptical."

Again with the arrogance. A sane person would sit meekly and hold their tongue. I want to poke him, see if I can get him to react.

"You don't think I can do it," I guess. "Is that why you won't look at me?"

"No," he says patiently as if explaining things to a small child. "I'm not looking at you because you're not properly clothed."

"You certainly couldn't get enough of me when I was naked," I mutter.

His gaze snaps to mine. "What did you say?"

"You heard me."

"You accuse me of peeping—"

"Peeping, no. Staring with your jaw on the floor, yes."

"That is not what I was—"

"You were practically drooling. Admit it."

For a moment we glare at each other, swords drawn. A red flush has crept across the duke's cheeks, and his dark eyes flash fire. Then he settles back in his chair. "Very well, Miss…"

"Beaumonde."

"Miss Beaumonde, I did look my fill. How could I not, when you were stumbling around my home?"

"I wasn't stumbling. I was chasing Elvis!"

"You almost fell over at least twice."

"Are you insinuating that I'm clumsy?"

"No." A cold smile. "I'm stating it as fact."

"Oh, go to hell." I want to smack the smirk off his regal face. "I was right. You do have a rod up your ass." The duke's nostrils flare and I straighten in triumph. "Did they insert it at birth? Or at the School for Dukes?"

"Miss Beaumonde, you'd better watch your tongue."

"Or else?"

Before the duke can answer, Daniel pops back in, covered

cage in hand. He strides to Elvis, and holds his hand sideways to tempt the bird to perch.

After a second of hesitation, Elvis hops on, and Daniel maneuvers him easily into the cage. "Who's a pretty boy? That's right."

I clench my jaw, suddenly resentful of how easily Daniel handles the parrot I'm supposed to be pet-sitting.

"Well, Your Grace." Daniel turns to the duke. "Did you ask her?"

"No," I say. "Whatever it is, the answer's no."

Daniel looks back and forth between me and the duke, an amused look on his face. "You're not curious as to what it is?"

I fold my arms over my chest. I am curious, but I'd rather drink the green smoothie Elvis pooped in than admit it.

"Your Grace?" Daniel prompts.

His Grace shakes his head slightly.

"Fine. I'll do it." Daniel opens his mouth but the duke beats him to it, turning to me and grinding out, as if it's the last thing he wants to say, "Will you marry me?"

My mouth falls open. That is not what I expected.

Daniel inserts himself between us. "Your Grace, if I may?"

The duke throws up his hands. "Very well."

Daniel turns to me. "He needs a bride."

"I'm sure you can find someone to take him." I find my voice, and the sarcasm that's become my first defense. "He's easy on the eyes, even if he is a bit stuck up."

The duke's chair scrapes the floor as he turns away, muttering. I smirk to myself.

"He needs a bride who looks like this." Daniel pulls out a folder from his briefcase.

The duke makes a noise of protest and Daniel waves him down. "She might as well see it. Papers hit the street hours ago."

"This is you?" I ask the duke.

A tight nod.

"It was all a misunderstanding," Daniel says smoothly.

"Sure it is."

"In my role, I cannot have a hint of scandal. Outrageous behavior is something I cannot indulge in." The duke's eyes scroll down from my face to my body, naked under his suit jacket. "Unlike some."

Jerkhole! I bite back the insult, but he can read it in my glare.

"We want to smooth things over as quickly as possible," Daniel says. "Your help will speed things along. You'd be well rewarded."

I hold back a snort and cross my arms. "I'd have to be." To put up with *him*. I don't add the last part, but the duke's cold stare tells me he heard it.

"We would make it worth your while. And you don't have to actually marry him," Daniel continues. "An engagement is fine. And it wouldn't be forever. Just until Midsummer, and then you can lie low. A few months from now, you can announce your breakup." He spreads his hands, beaming at us, as if to say, *See? See how easy it would be?*

For a moment, I consider. Me, affianced to a duke. A perfect, smiling, shiny version of myself gliding along beside him. Him offering his arm, smiling when he introduced me to people. Looking at me with fondness instead of with the expression of cold annoyance he's wearing now.

You don't belong. The voice rises from my past. In another life, another time, a pale-faced lady literally clutches her pearls. *You think you could ascend to our set?* She spits, eyes bulging. *You will never be good enough. You will never be one of us.*

I swallow against the sudden nausea. My limbs feel frail

and weak, like they did in that dark room long ago, standing in front of the family that thought they were too good for me. But I'm not that naive girl anymore. I never will be again.

The butterflies in my stomach turn into dragons, spitting fire. I turn up my nose and give the duke a look of queenly disdain. He blinks. *Oh yeah, a taste of your own medicine.*

"Frankie?" Daniel queries.

"Y'all are insane. Do people around here smoke crack for breakfast? Is that what that green liquid is?" I scoot my chair back with a loud scraping sound, and rise. The two men rise with me. I try not to act startled at the old-fashioned manners. *They're treating me like an equal.* But I'm not going to let it change my mind.

Nose in the air, I stalk to the piano, where I grab my bathrobe. "Turn around, please," I order. Both men oblige, and I switch the suit jacket for my robe.

I drape the suit jacket over the chair. "Please get that dry cleaned and send me the bill." I stride to the door, grabbing Elvis' cage on the way. "I'm leaving."

"Miss Frankie, please—" Daniel's shoes slide on the polished wood floor as he chases after me.

"Let her go," the duke commands.

Despite his employer's wishes, Daniel reaches the door before I do. "I know it's unorthodox," he says, hand on the doorknob. "But do consider it."

"No way. No freaking way. I know all about..." My voice hitches for a second, and it makes me madder. "I know all about rich boys and their toys. How they break them."

Daniel's eyebrows bounce at my statement. I've said too much.

I muster up a bit of upper class snobbery and raise my chin. "I'd like to leave now."

"As you wish." Daniel bows and opens the door with a

flourish. I gather my robe around me with as much dignity as I can muster, and swan onto the deck.

I get no further than the deck stairs when a man jumps out of the bushes, the dark eye of a camera in front of his face.

rankie

A FLASH WHITES out my vision. I throw up a hand to shield my eyes.

"Come on, miss, give me a smile!" the photographer shouts, still snapping.

Blinking against the flash, I trip backwards, losing my grip on Elvis' cage. It clatters to the porch, thankfully landing upright. Elvis squawks.

"Who are you?" Flash. "Are you the duke's lover?" Flash. "How long has this been going on?"

"Stop." I throw up my arm.

He doesn't stop. The shutter sounds intensify, and I realize my bathrobe has gaped open. I duck and wrench it closed, but before I can decide whether to run and abandon Elvis, I'm tugged against a firm chest. I startle, rearing back to fight until I hear the duke's deep voice.

"It's all right."

Despite myself, I sag in his strong arms. The Duke of New Arcadia's holding me close. Again. And it feels amazing.

"No comment," he thunders. His large hand cradles the side of my head, blocking my face from view. "This is private property. Leave before I call the Guard."

A quick pivot, and cool air hits my face. The duke has maneuvered us back inside into the blissful quiet.

"Oh my god," I say. I'm wobbly, and no matter how many times I blink, my surroundings are blurry. The duke steadies me, and then catches me up in his arms.

"Wait, I protest. "Elvis—"

"Daniel's got him." The duke carries me into a smaller, more private room, and sets me down onto a loveseat.

I tuck myself into the corner and press my hands to my face.

Gentle fingers brush my hair back. "Are you all right?"

I lower my hands and meet the duke's dark eyes. He sounds so different from before, so considerate and gentle. I wouldn't believe it was him if I weren't looking at him with my own eyes.

"I'm fine. It was just a shock." I gather my robe around me more tightly. "They saw me, though." I gulp. "They saw me naked."

The duke presses his lips together and his dark gaze goes arctic. A chill runs through me. "We will do everything we can to stop them."

"Of course we will." Daniel comes in and sets Elvis' cage beside the couch. The cage is covered and Elvis is quiet. After the excitement of this morning, he's probably sleeping.

"I've already texted the lawyers," Daniel continues. "And the Guard—"

"No," the duke commands. "They'll do an official report, and we don't want this getting out."

"I called an officer I know. He's discreet. And we'll

arrange for private security. But the situation as we know it has compounded." Daniel gives me a meaningful look before darting out of the room, his phone to his ear.

"What does that mean?" I pant. For some reason, my heart's revving and I'm out of breath. "What did he mean by that?"

The duke shakes his head, drawing a blanket over me. If he'd tried this ten minutes ago, I'd have knocked his hands away and snarked at him, but right now, I'm enjoying him fussing over me. His elegant hands smooth the blanket over my body.

Maybe he's not a spoiled rich boy. I push the hopeful thought away.

"Here." He leaves and heads to a small table graced with a tall decanter. He pours amber liquid into a fancy, heavy crystal glass, and returns. "Drink this."

I sniff it. The whiff of alcohol scorches my nostrils. "I don't know if this is a good idea."

"Just a bit," the duke orders, tipping the glass towards my mouth.

I frown over the rim. "You're bossy."

"Yes. Now, drink. Settle your nerves."

"I'm not a child." I can hear the petulance in my voice, but his orders make me want to argue.

"Good. I wouldn't serve a child good brandy."

"I'm not weak, either."

His lip twitches. A start of smile? "No, Miss Beaumonde. You are anything but weak."

I give in. He really is being kind. "Just Frankie. You can call me Frankie, too." I try a swallow, and sputter. The duke settles beside me. For all his lean build and finely tailored clothes, he's big and heavy up close. His hand rubs my back as I catch my breath.

"More," he commands.

"You just can't stop giving orders, can you?" But I obey. The duke remains by my side as the spirit singes my tongue. It burns less going down the second time, and warmth blooms through my stomach. "That's intense." I hand him the glass. "Good alcohol is wasted on me. I hope that wasn't expensive."

"Several hundred ducats," he says, the corner of his mouth pulling into faint parentheses before he smooths his expression.

I almost choke. Ducats are dollars. "Oh no."

"That was what it cost when my grandfather bought the bottle," he says. "Now it's worth much more. Priceless, I'd say."

I must look horrified because he adds, "It's all right, Frankie." He raises a hand slowly and smoothes back my hair. "It's worth it."

"To settle my nerves?" I must be feeling the effects of the alcohol, because my body feels loose. I relax deeper into the couch, enjoying the solid wall of the duke's body at my side, and his soft touch on my face.

He lowers his hand but stays close. I'm not sure he even realizes he touched me.

"I'm not a Victorian lady. I'm not going to faint." I eye the loveseat. "This isn't a fainting couch, is it?"

A ghost of a chuckle, but it lights up my nerve endings, singing through me like the clang of a bell. The duke's face is beautiful, lit by a reluctant laugh. "No. It's thoroughly modern."

"Mmm. Good. I'm not the fainting type. Though Victorian ladies weren't, either—they only did that because they were wearing corsets that constricted their breathing."

"Ah," he says, so seriously, I know he's inwardly amused.

I raise my chin. "Don't do that. Don't condescend."

He lifts his hands in surrender. And I know I'm really

feeling that priceless booze because I lay my head down on the back of the couch, close to his. When he does the same and turns his head, we're mere inches apart. His eyes are the color of espresso.

"Do you have a first name? Or does everyone just call you Duke?"

"They call me, 'Your Grace.'"

"Not, 'Your Majesty'?"

"No, only the queen is referred to as 'Your Majesty.' If I was a prince, it would be 'Your Highness.'"

"Your Highness," I say. Our faces are close enough together, I feel the puff of his huffed laugh on my skin.

"Not, 'Your Highness.' Simply 'Your Grace.'" A pause, then he adds softly, "My name is Benedict."

"Benedict." I mimic his upper-crust accent. "That's a very proper name."

"Indeed."

A line from a play drifts through my head and springs onto my tongue. *"Is it possible disdain should die while she hath such meet food to feed it as Signior Benedick?"* I quote in an Emma Thompson accent.

The duke's forehead knots. His breath wafts over my lips as he asks, "Pardon?"

"Never mind." I can't help lifting a hand and stroking his face, much like he did mine. His eyes go round with shock, then hood with another emotion.

"Soft," I say. "Your beard is softer than I imagined."

"Your Grace," Daniel calls, his voice breaking through the haze.

The duke's fingers close around my wrist and he gently pulls my hand away. But he doesn't let go. Daniel must notice, but he doesn't say anything.

"I'm good. I'm sober." I struggle upright. The duke helps me straighten, but stays at my side.

"She's had a shock," he tells Daniel.

"Indeed." Daniel frowns.

"Oh, for goodness sake, I'm fine." I tug back my hair. I feel ridiculous sitting in my bathrobe with two exquisitely dressed men, but what else is new? It's not the worst thing to happen this morning.

"All right." Daniel paces. "We must confer."

"Go ahead," the duke—Benedict—commands. I try to take my hand back, but his grip tightens. His thumb soothes the inside of my wrist.

"The photographers have been removed from the premises, and the security team is on their way. The lawyers are working on pressing charges to stop the most recent photos getting out. However, there's more press outside. Parked on the street."

"How many more?" Benedict demands.

"Five vans, six cars."

I stiffen, and the duke's arm goes around my shoulders. "We'll escort you home."

"That won't stop the scrutiny," Daniel says to me, almost apologetic. "They are calling you a mystery woman. I'm afraid the paparazzi won't stop until they know who you are."

Hot and cold race up my spine. I swallow. "I have nothing to hide," I lie.

"We will do our best to stop them," Benedict vows. He glances back at Daniel.

"Of course we will. However, there's no doubt this complicates things. First the pictures, then an unknown woman of similar description exiting your house in the buff."

"It's my problem," Benedict says. His left hand has moved to my back, and it rubs up and down. "I don't want to drag Frankie into it."

"No, wait," I protest. "I'm an adult. I can handle it. I want to help."

"What Daniel's proposing is ludicrous," Benedict says. His deep voice rumbles through my body. The sensation is delicious. I try not to lose my train of thought.

"But… could we pull it off?" I ask.

Daniel arches a brow at me, and I realize I'm sitting on the couch, holding the duke's hand with his arm around me.

"I mean," I swallow and will my blush not to rise, "is it possible that, if we announce our engagement, the paparazzi will back off?"

"No," Benedict says at the same time as Daniel says, "Yes."

"With permission, Your Grace?" Daniel waits for a nod from the duke before he launches into his plan. "I believe if we announce it soon, we can shape the narrative. You're the commoner next door, he met you when you were pet sitting. We stick to the truth. It could work."

The duke snorts.

"It could," Daniel insists.

"But I'm American. Won't that be a problem?"

Daniel waves a hand. "We'll deal with that later. It's not like you actually have to marry him."

"Well, thank god for that," I say, mostly joking, but the duke stiffens.

"Excuse me," he says, removing his hand.

"Eligible royals falling in love with Americans is in vogue," Daniel says. "It would be a scandal, yes, but minor. And it would deflect from the actual scandal."

"Would it?" I ask.

The duke sighs. "I suppose it would."

"You know I'm right." Daniel is almost crowing.

I narrow my eyes at him. "Not so fast, Fairy Godfather. When I said I'm American, I meant I have zero idea what royal protocol is. I have no idea how to act."

"Easily taught." Daniel shrugs.

"I must be drunk." I shake my head. "I can't believe I'm considering this." But I am considering it. I've been burned before, but maybe the duke isn't like those assholes. The duke is… almost nice.

"Is it so inconceivable to consider?" Daniel asks, sweeping his arms out. "Look at him!"

I do as instructed and turn to behold Benedict.

"Tall. Handsome. Intelligent." Daniel ticks his boss's attributes off using his fingers. "Did I mention tall?"

"Daniel," Benedict warns.

"And… he's rich." Daniel glares at the duke. I feel like I'm in the middle of a fight. "So whatever you would like, Frankie, ask now."

"Anything?" I ask Benedict. "Up to half your kingdom?" I quip.

"My god." Benedict touches a finger to his head, like Daniel and my shenanigans are giving him a headache. St. Francis save me, I love seeing him squirm.

"Money?" Daniel suggests. "Connections? Citizenship?"

I suck in a breath. Citizenship in New Arcadia is seriously hard to get. You have to prove Arcadian ancestry going back three generations.

"You could officially immigrate here." Daniel dangles the bait. "And we could set you up with whatever you need. A house? A car?"

"A scholarship? Or money, so I could go to university?" The University of Arcadia is close to here. I passed it in a cab on the way from the airport. The towering gothic structure surrounded by cherry trees in bloom is the epitome of a hallowed hall of learning. I could go there, graduate, and get a job. I'd never have to leave. I'd be a success, and I'd never have to return home.

"Done." Daniel doesn't smile, but his eyes shine.

Benedict clears his throat. "Excuse us, Miss Beaumonde," he says. "I need a word with my head of PR."

The two stalk out of the room, leaving me huddled on the couch, gnawing my lip. What the hell is happening here? One minute, I'm enjoying coffee and contemplating a quiet year. The next, I'm considering stepping out of my solitude to fake an engagement with a man dogged by paparazzi. I might have to rub elbows with awful, judgy rich people—and worse. *Royal* rich people.

I start to bite my lip and then stop. No more nervous habits. No more weird tics. I will have to dress properly, act properly. Half the time, I don't even remember to brush my hair. What the hell am I thinking?

"Miss Beaumonde." Benedict is back, and for some reason I feel relief. It's as if the room stops spinning.

He seats himself next to me, and I automatically align myself to him, leaning close. He leans in too, putting his hand on my knee. "I know this is very sudden."

My heart flutters despite itself. He looks so serious and handsome, my toes curl like a nervous bride's. "Are you going to propose?"

His lips quirk. God, he's so pretty. "It's not ideal, I know. I'm the last person you would consider marrying."

"More like the other way around." I wrinkle my nose.

"I'd marry you," he says immediately, then gives his head a little shake when he realizes what he just said. " Or someone like you. That is to say—"

"I get it," I say, then flush. "Sorry. I shouldn't interrupt. I'll have to break that habit." I fold my hands in my lap. Calm. Poised. Meek. Demure.

Argh, this is not going to work.

"So you'd do it?" Benedict asks.

I start to shrug, and stop myself. Geez, faking all this

poise makes me feel like a mannequin. "I feel responsible for some of this mess."

"It's hardly your fault."

"I know. But getting caught on camera on your porch hardly helped."

Benedict takes my hand. Little tingles run up my arm. "If we do this, I'll be able to shield you better. The paparazzi can be vicious, but I can call on my connections, make it clear that, as my fiancée, you're off limits."

I stare at our interlaced fingers. My insides are shifting, rearranging.

"I will take care of it, Frankie. I promise." He squeezes my hand. "I will take care of you."

My last bit of backbone melts. Those long eyelashes, his strong hand squeezing mine, his sincere tone—there's no way I can say no now. I lick my lips, and his gaze falls to my mouth.

"What about… a trial run? See if I can do it?" I say.

"I know you can." Again, the instant vote of confidence. I have definitely fallen into some sort of fairytale. Guys who are this perfect do not exist.

I squeeze the duke's hand. He definitely exists. And he's not totally perfect. He's as arrogant as they come—I stand by my first assessment. But in the past half hour, he's been kind. I've been on my own so long, I can't resist the chance to have someone care for me.

"All right," I whisper. "I'll do it. I'll try."

"Are you sure?" Benedict's face is very close to mine. Beyond him, I see Daniel waiting in the doorway, watching us intently.

I nod. "I want to help. I'll do my best."

"Excellent," Daniel says, coming into the room. Benedict and I break apart but keep holding hands as Daniel rubs his palms together. "Operation Fake Fiancée Phase One is a go."

* * *

Frankie

"So you're actually going to do it?" my friend Mina asks via our web chat.

I lean back in the black leather recliner. In front of me, a black and white movie plays with the sound off. Katherine Hepburn strides in front of the camera, arguing with Jimmy Stuart and Cary Grant. Elvis sits on a special perch beside me, shifting from claw to claw, doing a little birdy dance. When the camera zooms in on Cary Grant, the bird fluffs his feathers and dances faster.

"I don't know, Mina," I say. "I feel like it's my fault."

A cascade of clacking computer keys is the background music to Mina's snort. "No way is it your fault. These celebrity types make their own beds."

"He's not a celebrity. He's a duke. I looked it up—he's in line to be a prince. Like, runner up to king."

"Whatever." Mina's tone is flat, unimpressed. "I'm American."

"So am I! It's just... being around him, I can tell he's... different. Used to being in charge." I press my hands to my face. I'm a mess.

"Silver spoon stuck up his ass?" Once again, Mina is a mood I wish I could channel.

It's my turn to snort. "I may have said something to that effect."

"Whoa, Frankie. Good for you." Only Mina would be so admiring of downright rudeness.

"It was in the heat of the moment," I mumble. "I thought he was annoying." I'm out of my head around him. Considering I live most of my life in my head, this is new territory.

"So he's annoying, stuck up, bossy, and you still want to marry him?"

"I'm going to pose as his fiancée. Totally different."

"If you say so." More typing on Mina's end. I've never had a conversation with her that wasn't accompanied by constant typing. Total code-addict, but she always keeps up her end of the conversation. "Knowing these royals, there'll be all sorts of hoops you'll have to jump through."

"Yeah, I'll have to have lessons. It'll make Grandmère's finishing classes look like a cakewalk."

"Not a carrot walk?" Mina asks in a sly tone.

"Har. Har." I rub my face and push back my thick mass of hair. "I never should've told you about that particular incident."

A chuckle, and the typing reaches epic speeds. "I assume it'll come out to your new fiancé."

"Ugh. yes. They're going to vet me tomorrow. They need to know everything. By the way," I add, "this conversation is completely confidential. You can't tell anyone about this. They'll have me sign an NDA… I just needed to run this by someone."

"And you know I'd never talk. I never talk to anyone if I can help it. There are only like three people in this world I can stand. Maybe four."

I roll my eyes, but I know she's serious. "Yeah, well, me too."

"Figured. Why else would you have moved to another country to live in a giant empty house with only a parrot to talk to?"

I forgot I didn't really tell Mina why I left my hometown. Why I ran so far away. I swallow, and try to keep my tone light. "Don't forget the creepy artwork."

The typing stops. "Is that why you're doing it?"

"What do you mean?" I rub my forehead. It's weird to talk to Mina when her keyboard is silent.

"You're agreeing to become someone's fake fiancée. Why?" Like a shark scenting blood in the water. I should have known better than to hide from my best friend. My only friend. The only reason Mina doesn't run the world is because 'adulting', as she calls it, makes her bored.

"The money, obviously." I stick with the most likely explanation. "It's enough to pay for me to go to college. You know I always wanted to do that, but my parents could never afford it. And the duke offered me citizenship. On top of making the paparazzi pictures go away." I shudder. I'd hate for Grandmère to hear the story of how I ended up cornered —naked—on a duke's porch. Not that Grandmère pays attention to foreign news, but I'm from a small town. Someone would forward it to someone, and within hours, everyone would know.

"But won't this put you even more in the spotlight?" Mina continues. "I can't imagine what it would be like, being the American wife of a crown prince. Possibly future king. Is it even legal?"

I've twined my hair on my finger so tightly, it's stuck. I tug it free, frowning at the sting. "We're not actually getting married. I think a future king actually marrying an immigrant is frowned upon. Benedict would never let anything keep him from the line of succession."

"Oh, *Benedict*, is it?" Mina's tone switches from intense to an unsubtle purr. "On a first name basis, are we?"

"He told me his name, but I'm supposed to call him 'Your Grace'."

"Even in bed?"

"Mina!" I snap upright so fast, Elvis nearly falls off his perch. "It's not going to get that far." I cup the phone and whisper as if Elvis is eavesdropping, "I'm not going to sleep with him."

"If you say so. He's pretty easy on the eyes."

"Did you look him up?" I bite my lip, remembering the way his suit pants stretched across his tight rear.

"Looking at him now. Very, very nice." Mina purrs. "He's got that goatee look down."

"It definitely works for him. And damn but he can wear a suit. Not that I'm attracted to him or anything."

"Of course not."

I frown at her mocking tone. "It's fake, Mina. All fake. I'm just going to do this as… a favor. Another job, like pet sitting."

Mina snickers. "More like duke sitting."

"Oh my god." I cover my face. "No."

"The question is, are you sitting on his lap or his face—"

"Mina! Enough." I swallow, but it's no use. My cheeks are burning, and my belly fills with a lazy swell of desire. *I will take care of you,* the duke said, his voice soft and strong and swoonworthy. Almost enough to make me rethink my opinion of spoiled rich guys.

"Frankie and the duke, sitting in a tree. F-U-C-K-I-N—"

"My god, Mina, how old are you? Stop!" I sputter. We aren't… that's not… we're not going to do anything. This is a fake engagement. In name only. No touching. Definitely no sitting. On faces or laps." I'll chalk up our moment on the couch to the priceless brandy.

Mina stops laughing. "If you say so. You're only his until the stroke of midnight, and all that?"

"Exactly."

Mina hits a few more keys before answering, "All right, Cinderella. Be sure to hang on to your shoes."

rankie

DANIEL RINGS the doorbell precisely at nine a.m.

"Ah," he says when I open the door. "Miss Beaumonde. You look ravishing."

I roll my eyes, and give a little curtsey.

"But your curtsey needs work." Daniel struts past me, looking extra fine in a mustard-colored suit, and narrow white ankle boots. Not many men could pull off that shade of yellow, but the color makes his dark brown skin glow. "And where's Elvis this fine morning?"

"Locked in the jungle room."

"Good, good. Where shall we hold our little tête-à-tête?"

"In the kitchen?" Already I'm feeling small and drab compared to Daniel. I am properly dressed and wearing a bra, which is more than I can say most days. "I can make coffee."

"Lead the way. We'll start with the vetting. Assuming

everything goes well, we'll move on to wardrobe and etiquette."

"Full day," I mutter.

"Darling, you have no idea. If you check out, I'm going to turn your entire life upside down. It'll be grueling, but quite something to put on your resume. Except you can't, because of the NDA."

"Got it." I spread my hands. "Ask your questions. I've got nothing to hide."

"How boring." Daniel drums his fingers on the counter. "I do hope you have at least some naughty skeletons in the armoire."

"Nope."

His eyes narrow. "Hmmm."

* * *

Frankie

"So let me get this straight," Daniel asks, eyes on his clipboard. "Only child, small town, straight A student. Mother passed away, father still living. One boyfriend for six months after you turned eighteen. No college. You moved out and supported yourself by pet-sitting."

"Yes. I started working as a dog walker and got a reputation for being good with animals. When someone invited me to spend a month in their home watching their dog, I did it. My business grew from there."

"You move around and stay in people's homes and watch their pets while they travel." Daniel makes a note.

"Exactly. I have lots of references, if you need them." I start to make a joke about a duke being easier to babysit than a mule or a ball python, but shut my mouth. Comparing one's fake fiancé to an ass or a snake is probably impolite.

48

"Moving from city to city and living alone with different animals must be hell on your social life," Daniel muses.

"What social life?" I twist my lips. "I have a large collection of classic movies."

"What made you take this job in New Arcadia?"

"Um, I always wanted to visit?" I shrug. "Lady Drey liked my references and got it into her mind I was the best person to watch Elvis. She handled the visa." Daniel's dark eyes keep probing, and I resist the urge to squirm. "I like to travel. I grew up in a small town and never thought I'd have the money to see the world." I've glossed over a bit, and I'm hoping Daniel doesn't pry too closely. He's so cosmopolitan, maybe he'll assume I couldn't stand small town living.

"But since coming here, you've kept to yourself. You've barely left this house since moving into the country."

"Yes." I shift on my seat. Where is he going with this?

"It's official." Daniel sets down the clipboard on which he's made copious notes on every memory and moment of my life. "You are the most boring person on the face of the Earth."

"That's not true!" I protest. "I'm a very interesting person. I have lots of vices!"

"No lovers." Daniel ticks off his fingers. "No friends. No family. At least not that you keep up with."

"I have an online friend; I told you about her."

Daniel waves a hand, dismissing Mina. "You, my dear, are a recluse. And how I love you for it."

"Excuse me?"

"It's perfect. No one has seen you. No one knows where you are. I can invent any story about you, and people will believe it."

I shift on my stool. "You sound like a serial killer."

"I'm not going to kill you, darling. I'm going to make you a star. Well, a star-crossed lover. You saw the duke from afar, and wanted him. Then, Fate intervened in the form of a parrot, and romance was born."

"So you think we should do it?" I tilt my coffee cup this way and that, studying the dregs. Are coffee grounds like tea leaves? Can they tell the future?

Daniel takes my hands and leans close. "I think we should not waste this golden opportunity. An engagement will clear the duke's name, and put the spotlight where it should be."

"But it would all be fake."

"Just the teensy tiniest bit fake." Daniel shrugs. "Like a play. Have you ever acted before?"

"I did a one woman act for the Miss Carrot Pageant. An abbreviated version of Shakespeare's *Much Ado About Nothing*. It was my talent."

"A one woman act of *Much Ado About Nothing*," Daniel repeats slowly. "I have so many questions. What's the Miss Carrot Pageant?"

"I told you about it." I gesture at his clipboard. "The beauty contest I entered when I was fifteen."

"There's a beauty contest called the Miss *Carrot* Pageant?" Daniel wildly pages through his notes.

"It's a thing," I insist. "Believe me, I wish it wasn't. My mother won it when she was fifteen. So did my Grandmère —my father's mother. And two of my cousins. I didn't want to enter, but it's tradition."

"And did you win?"

"No. Didn't come close." I don't want any more coffee but I raise my mug enough to hide my smirk as I add, "We wore green wigs and orange dresses. To look like carrots."

"Sweet baby Jesu," Daniel's clipboard clatters to the counter as he sways in his chair.

I set my mug down. "Are you okay? You seriously look like you're going to faint."

"I need a moment. The thought of all those young ladies dressed in…"

"Carrot costumes."

"Oh," Daniel groans.

"Do you need smelling salts? I'm sure there are some around here somewhere, New Arcadian types being so faint prone." I can't stop my laugh. After my fit of giggles, Daniel catches on and glares at me. "You were joking."

"Of course I was. Come on. Grant County is small, but we're not that backward."

"I wouldn't put it past the States to do anything. They call crisps 'chips.' And chips 'flies.'"

"Fries," I correct. "And how is that backward? Never mind."

"So you weren't wearing the green wig and orange dress?"

"Nope. I was wearing a purple dress. My mother's old dress. There are purple carrots, you know."

"No, I didn't know. I could've gone a lifetime and never missed knowing that. Or about Miss Carrot competitions in Smallville, USA."

"Grant Town, USA. Named for Mr. Grant, famed carrot farmer."

"Of course." Daniel picks up his clipboard. "And why didn't you win?"

"You really want to know?"

He nods.

"I was wearing high heels—but they were too big for me. They were my cousin's."

"Go on."

"It was an accident. I mean, it was almost inevitable that I would fall over, wearing those things. But I grabbed what I could on the way down and… it happened to be Betty Jo's hairdo."

"Oh no." Daniel's eyes close.

"Fortunately, Betty Jo was wearing a wig. Unfortunately, it came free and I kept falling—and grabbed Donna Draper's dress." I wince, remembering. "It wasn't properly sewn, only pinned. So it… well, it ripped off."

"My god."

"Yeah, it was bad. The judges had to disqualify me. I took out two contestants in one fall. That, combined with the thing on the float—"

"What thing on the float?" Daniel looks pained to ask.

"I knocked a girl off." My nonchalant wave brushes my coffee mug and sends it dancing off the counter's edge. Daniel catches it. "She was fine. Her wrist healed, eventually."

Daniel replaces the coffee mug carefully onto the counter, away from me. "Frankie, darling, I mean this in the nicest way possible. You are a walking, talking harbinger of mayhem."

"I don't mean to be." I pretend to pout, secretly glad he's not calling me boring anymore.

Daniel has his head in his hands, rubbing his face. "And I am going to let you become affianced to my esteemed employer."

"You mean it?" I sit up on my bar chair, almost knocking the coffee cup over again. "We're going through with it?"

"Against my better sense." Daniel drags his hands down and wags a finger in my face. "The fate of the country rests on the veracity of this engagement."

"I understand." I fold my hands in my lap and look as serious and trustworthy as I can. "I won't let you down."

Daniel opens his mouth, but before he can say anything, there's a giant clatter in the hallway. Like someone knocked over a rack of pots and pans.

"What was that?" Daniel asks. "It sounded like a car crash. Is this house haunted?"

"Oh no." I shoot to my feet and rush down the hall.

There's Benedict on the floor, grappling with the suit of armor. Sir Fred's arm is extended, but his spear and gauntlet lie on the ground.

"Your Grace!" Daniel shouts. Together, we all manage to lift the suit of armor off the duke. "My god, what happened?"

"It just jumped out at me. Nearly impaled me on this thing." The duke pushes at the spear.

"He does that," I say apologetically. "I call him Sir Fred." I face dual blank stares, and explain. "Ancestor of Freddy Krueger. Always jumping out at people."

"Sir Fred," Daniel says thoughtfully.

"A little help here?" Benedict demands.

Together, Daniel and the duke wrestle the suit of armor back into place. Daniel shoves the final metal glove onto the arm piece, but sets the spear aside. "There. Now, Your Grace, were you hurt?"

"Just a flesh wound," the duke mutters, touching his eye. By the time Daniel is examining it in the better light in the kitchen, a slight bruise has formed.

"Oh dear," Daniel murmurs, touching the discolored skin. The duke is stoic but I wince for him. "We'll have to fix that with makeup." Daniel darts this way and that, studying the bruise from different angles. "With your permission, Your Grace."

"Yes, fine," Benedict growls, and waves Daniel away.

"We can't have people saying your fiancée knocks you about," Daniel adds, his cheek curving as he glances at his phone and scuttles out of the room. "Be right back."

The duke glowers at the giant lemon paintings, brushing off invisible specks of dust from his suit. As usual, he looks ready for a Hugo Boss photoshoot. With his face and build a perfect balance of strong and lean, he'd do the fashion line a favor.

I forgot how handsome he is in person. All the flattering

photos of him Mina found fall short. It's not just his looks. It's something else. A presence. He feels three times as large as anyone else I've ever met.

Normally, this would make me run and hide, but with him, I can't stop myself inching forward.

"Are you okay?" I ask. "I'm sorry the house attacked you. It takes some getting used to."

"Mmm." The duke nods to the oil paintings. "My great aunt collects art like this. Garish stuff." He flicks his gaze to me. "I see you're wearing clothes today."

I mock curtsey. "All for you, Your Highness." I ladle out as much sarcasm as I can.

"The proper term is 'Your Grace'."

"Even in bed?" Gah! *Stop, mouth!*

"Bed?" He turns fully to face me. "We won't be sharing a bed."

"Of course not," I backtrack. *Damn you, Mina.* I can hear her cackling. "I wouldn't sleep with you if you paid me."

"Good. I won't be paying you," the duke half scoffs, half sneers.

"Not for service in bed, anyway," I snap back. *Fuck you, Benedict.* "Actually, I have a question."

"Ask." He makes an invitation sound like a command. We face off like Western gunfighters.

"The queen hasn't named an heir since her sister died." I pause, remembering that the queen's sister was Benedict's late mother, but he doesn't look particularly grieved. He raises his chin, almost bored.

"What of it?"

"I'm wondering why all the pomp and ceremony. Aren't you automatically her heir?"

"Not until she makes it official."

"But why?"

"It's tradition." Benedict's voice is heavy with unspoken

commentary: *stupid foreign commoner, asking silly questions.* It makes me want to strangle him with his own silk tie. "I wouldn't expect an American to understand."

"Oh, tone down the condescension. My traditions are different, not stupid."

Benedict blinks. "Fair enough."

I blink at the change in his tone. I didn't expect him to listen and change his behavior.

"It's tradition dating back hundreds of years. Before your country even existed," he adds with a touch of arrogance. "It's written into our laws. The ruling monarch must make an official announcement of their heir apparent. This allows lords and other branches of government to accept or issue a formal challenge."

"A challenge? Like a duel?"

"Yes." Benedict's dry tone balances my excitement. "Exactly like that. The challenged gets to choose the weapon of choice. We've had jousts, sword fighting, even a schnitzel eating contest."

"So cool."

"Indeed. I'm glad my country's customs amuse you," he says, proving sarcasm isn't a weapon reserved only for me.

"So why hasn't she officially named you as heir? Why now?"

"The queen is pregnant. If all goes well, god willing, it behooves her to name an heir as regent in case something happens to her while her children are young."

I want to stop asking questions, but I can't. "But why now? Why not before?"

"When my mother died, I was twelve. She couldn't name me heir then."

I persist. "But why not when you came of age?"

He shakes his head slightly, looking... not annoyed, but tired. "We had hoped the queen would conceive. Failing that, she would have named an heir on her fiftieth birthday." His answers leave much to be desired.

"All right then, next question. Why aren't you already married?"

"It's a good thing he isn't." Daniel sails back into the room and inserts himself between us. "Otherwise this little ruse would never work."

"You're so sure it will?" the duke asks without taking his eyes off me.

"Give me twenty-four hours," Daniel says.

"You have twelve." With one last derisive glance at me, the duke turns on his heel and strides out of the kitchen.

"Jerkhole," I breathe. "Did he just come over to insult me?"

"Probably to check on progress." Daniel clears the coffee cups and puts them into the dishwasher. "You fascinate him."

"What?" I sputter.

Daniel wipes his hand on a cloth and carefully replaces it before turning to me. "Are you ready for the next stage of this theatrical performance?"

My hand flies to my neck. "What, now?"

"Hair and wardrobe are here. Just let them in."

Between Daniel and the duke's visit, I feel like Dorothy being spun around in a tornado. "Vetting is over?"

"Your part. I have people working to corroborate everything you told me. But you heard the duke. I have twelve hours. It's time to get my fairy godmother on."

"All right. I'm ready." I gulp and add more firmly, "Turn this pumpkin into a princess. Or rather, carrot into a duchess."

"Very well, my Lady Carrot." He grins and offers me his arm. "Let's bibbity bobbity boo."

* * *

Frankie

"The Queen is 'Your Majesty'," Daniel says. "Crown princes are 'Your Highness'."

"But there are no crown princesses," I say, focusing on putting one foot in front of the other. It's harder than it would normally be, because I'm wearing four-inch heels and have a giant book balanced on my head.

"Not yet. Once His Grace is crowned, he will be in line for the throne." Daniel pauses. "You're quite good at this."

I execute a smooth turn and strut back the way I came, the book still perfectly balanced. "Grandmère made us run drills like this. Posture, balance, poise. My cousins were always better than I." I forget myself and shrug, and the book thunks to the floor.

Daniel clears his throat.

"Sorry." I grab the huge tome. "I'll keep practicing."

"I'd recommend it. You can memorize the lists of peers, their histories and titles while you do. I suggest copying details out of Kingman's Peerage, and making flashcards."

"What's Kingman's Peerage?"

"It's a book."

"Can I have a copy?"

Daniel looks pointedly at the giant book I'm already holding. The cover says 'Kingman's Book of Peers' in such grandiose script, I can barely read it. I open it with a sigh, but Daniel grabs my arm before I can see a word.

"Not now, darling. Time for your makeover. Then we practice curtseys."

Over the next two hours, I'm plucked, shaved, waxed, and buffed.

"Is all this really necessary?" I whine to Daniel as he oversees the stylist trimming my hair.

"You're entering a new world. You will be judged at first

appearance. It'll be bad enough when you open your mouth and everyone learns you're American—"

"Hey!"

"But as long as you look like you come from old money, you'll be fine." His eyes narrow. "I do have a question. While we're on the subject of money, why don't you like spoiled rich boys?"

I open my mouth but my brain hasn't caught up with the subject change. "What? I mean, pardon me?"

Daniel waves a hand. "You mentioned spoiled rich boys, and your tone was firmly derisive. I only want to understand. Spoiled rich boys are my favorite." He gives a little smile.

I knew it. I knew someone who paired a mustard suit with white boots and a cravat wasn't totally straight. I tell Daniel this and he laughs. "I'm bi, actually. But you haven't answered my question."

Darn it. "Um, I grew up in a small town, right? But it was close to this world famous resort. It's the big employer in the area. If you don't want to farm carrots, you work there." Like my parents did, all their lives. Like I would have if I hadn't gotten out. "It's super fancy, thousands of dollars a night. A lot of rich people come there and… well, their kids weren't so nice to those of us who lived in town."

"Ah," Daniel says knowingly. Maybe he's been around the upper crust enough to see kids in Versace's resort wear behaving like bullies. "And your parents worked there, correct?"

"Yes," I say, and leave it at that. Thankfully, he doesn't pry.

The stylist steps back and Daniel motions me to stand in front of a full-length mirror. I go nervously to take a look.

"Oh… wow." A brand shiny new and improved Frankie Beaumonde looks back. My hair is still long, but cut expertly so layers fall below my shoulders. A few subtle highlights brighten my face, making me look younger and more sophisticated at the same time. My thick eyebrows have been bush-whacked into respectable arches, and my nails are neat and shiny, polished in a nude color that matches my skin tone. The effect is natural, but glamorous.

The woman looking back at me belongs in the halls of the rich and royal. At a thousand dollars a night resort.

"Classy and understated," Daniel says with satisfaction. "Next is wardrobe. Come."

* * *

CHAPTER 5

"And final fiduciary considerations include..." the finance minister's voice drones into nothing, and I force myself not to look at the grandfather clock ticking in the corner. My morning's meetings seem to take forever. I even found myself tapping a pen halfway through the quarterly budget review. I was fidgeting, and I never fidget.

"And therefore, we have determined Cawthorne holdings proposal will benefit our nation for decades to come. And therefore--"

If you say 'therefore' one more time...

At last the meeting comes to an end. My jaw aches from clenching it against yawns. Duty done, I rise and leave without more than a nod to any officials. I never was one for small talk, and Daniel gave me strict instructions not to talk to anyone until I've made a formal statement to the press about the leaked photos.

"Home, McKinney," I tell my driver, and bite my tongue several times to keep from urging him to drive faster.

"How goes it?" I ask Daniel as soon as he greets me at the door.

"It's going well. Better than I expected. At this rate, we'll meet your twelve hour deadline."

"Very good." I smooth my tie. "Of course, of you I had no doubt. And where is our Cinderella?"

"Back this way." Daniel waves for me to follow. "She's with the dance master now. You remember Monsieur Villiers?"

"Fondly," I say in a tone that indicates otherwise.

Daniel chuckles. "He's quite taken with our Frankie."

"Is he?" I dog Daniel's steps through the maze of antiques to a back parlor where his staff have moved the furniture aside to create a dance floor.

I hear her before I see her—a loud, lilting laugh, unfurling like a banner. Unraveling my poise. I brace myself for the sight of her.

And when I do, my feet stall. My body tightens, blood pounding downwards, leaving me light headed. They've put makeup on her, done her hair, but it's still Frankie. Her mouth is very, very red, her lips are wide, and she's laughing.

My brunette Venus spins this way and that, admiring the way the full skirt of her gown swishes over the floor. The lean dance master in his tuxedo gestures for her to complete a proper step, but she's ignoring him, dancing to the beat of her own DJ.

How is it possible for a woman to affect me like this? Last night, after she left, I took a cold shower that didn't help one bit. I finally gave in and took care of myself, picturing Frankie the whole time, and when I was done, I may as well have not done anything at all. I told myself it was a simple physical reaction, a byproduct of not having had sex in a long time. But Winnie Bennett, naked, literally throwing herself at me, didn't elicit the same amount of ardor as Frankie Beaumonde in my suit jacket, stumbling around my home and telling me to go to hell.

"Your Grace?" Daniel is waiting for me to catch up to him. I need to get hold of myself. "What do you think?"

I take another long look. "Is that her?" I swallow to hide a thickening in my voice and… other parts.

"It is indeed. Our ugly duckling turned into a swan."

"Better than a parrot." I can't tear my eyes away from Frankie as she glides across the makeshift dance floor, so I don't bother trying.

Daniel barks a laugh. "Why, Your Grace, you made a joke."

"Yes, well. I'm allowed one a quarter."

"And another. Fulfilling your yearly quota early."

"I'm an overachiever. Is she ready?"

"What's the rush?"

"Brunch with Lady Ursaline tomorrow."

"That old dragon? Does she know the truth?"

"No. She's the first test. If Frankie passes, this might have a shot at working."

On the dance floor, Frankie has finally allowed the dance master to lead her in a series of proper steps. Halfway through, she throws her head back and laughs in sheer delight at something the dance master says. He leads her into a series of tight turns, and Frankie follows beautifully, her dark hair flying.

"It doesn't have to be her," Daniel murmurs.

"What do you mean?"

"We could cut her loose, find another. Someone from New Arcadia; better pedigree."

"No." I try to imagine another taking Frankie's place, and

can't. Frankie's face is all I see—laughing, tipsy on the couch, telling me I have a rod up my ass. Protecting that godforsaken parrot. "I want her."

Daniel's perfect eyebrows shoot up so high, they'd reach his hairline if he had one.

"I want her to do it," I amend, though that's not much better. "I don't care about pedigree. She's smart. She can play the part. That's what matters."

"All right, Your Grace," Daniel says. "If you insist."

Frankie's laughter washes over me again. Now the dance master looks bemused, as if surprised to find he's having fun. Whenever Frankie tosses her head back to laugh, his gaze flicks to her breasts.

"Enough of this," I mutter, and stride forward. Monsieur Villiers jumps when I tap him on the shoulder. "I'm cutting in."

"Your Grace." Frankie steps back, dark eyes flashing. "What a surprise. And an honor." The way she says 'honor' indicates she means otherwise.

I extend a hand. "Dance with me."

"Please," she corrects. "Dance with me, *please*. It's a request, not a command. Or do dukes not say 'please'?"

"Dukes don't make requests."

Frankie rolls her eyes.

"Fine," she snaps and then turns to curtsey gracefully to Monsieur Villiers. "Thank you, sir."

"Pleasure is all mine, Miss Beaumonde." The dance master is all smiles now. "And if I might add, whoever taught you to dance gave you a good foundation—"

"Enough," I cut in, gathering Frankie in my arms. "Let's dance."

"Of course, Your Grace," Monsieur Villiers says.

"Rude," Frankie mutters.

"I beg your pardon?" I place a hand on her back and pull her in tighter. "Do you have something to say, Miss Beaumonde?"

"Oh come off it," she pushes at my shoulder, "I don't see why I have to pretend you're the paragon of good behavior when you act like an arrogant ass."

"I know which rules to follow, and which to toss aside."

"And everyone thinks whatever you do is proper because of your title."

"Exactly." The music starts, but before I can take a step, Frankie tugs at me. "Stop," I order. "I'm to lead."

"Get on with it then!" She glares up at me.

"Everything all right, Your Grace?" Daniel calls. He and his team have gathered on the edge, watching us.

"We have an audience," Frankie mutters.

"Hang on and follow my lead, Miss Beaumonde." I launch into the waltz before she can protest. If I had wanted to catch her off guard, I would have failed. She matches my steps perfectly—so smoothly, I'm speechless until we've danced across half the room. "You're not half bad."

"Thank you. My grandmother ran a cotillion. My cousins and I had to attend. Four years of dance and etiquette lessons."

I spin her, and she pivots smoothly. The second time, she grins; the third time, she laughs. We promenade down the room and back. I spin her again and again, and her smile socks me each time. But the best part is drawing her back into my arms.

"Your bruise looks better," she murmurs, angling her face close so she can study my eye socket.

"You should see the other guy," I whisper, and hold her close so I feel her laugh as it tickles my ear.

The song comes to an end. I keep us swaying, holding her

a second past the last orchestral note. Our audience applauds. Monsieur Villiers is beaming.

"That was fun, Benedict," Frankie says as Daniel comes up to us.

Daniel jolts. "She calls you, 'Benedict'?"

"Yes. It's my name." I raise my chin, daring further comment.

"Oh, I mean, 'Your Grace'." She rolls her eyes, as if my title was designed specifically to annoy her. She gives me a flawless curtsey—then crosses her eyes and sticks out her tongue.

A chuckle bursts from my chest before I can stop it. Frankie winks and sashays off to speak to the dance master.

Daniel studies me. "I've never heard you laugh before."

"Nonsense." I half turn to keep an eye on Frankie. She's talking fast, waving her hands, her whole face lit up. Monsieur Villiers looks like he's in heaven. "You must have heard me laugh before."

"Not like that." Daniel gives me a look, and hands me something small and square. A black velvet box. "Just had it delivered. A princess cut diamond, white gold band. You ready?"

A tremor runs through me. I grip the box tighter, just in case. "Of course." I turn to where Daniel's staff has formed a circle around Frankie. My presumptive fiancée is holding court as if she was born to do it.

"Miss Beaumonde, a word?" I call to her.

Daniel leans close. "Be nice," he warns.

I give him a look.

Frankie scampers up. With her flushed cheeks and hair escaping its ringlets, she looks more like a girl playing dress up than a sophisticated deb ready to attend a ball. And I adore her for it. "You rang?" she says.

"A little privacy, please." I frown at Daniel, who nods.

"Ah yes." He raises his arm and snaps his fingers. "Everyone, out. Thank you, thank you, well done, good job. You too, Monsieur Villiers. Come, come." Daniel herds everyone from the room.

I turn to Frankie, who is fidgeting with her skirts. "How was your day?"

"Long." She tucks a strand of hair behind her ear. "Are we doing what fiancés would do? Making small talk? Is that why you're being polite?"

"I am always polite."

"Talking to me like I'm a person instead of a naughty dog." She wrinkles her nose at me. I have to clench my fist to stop from reaching for her.

"I don't know." I lower my voice. "You are quite naughty." I shouldn't say it. I'm losing control of myself, and I am always in control.

She blinks at me, then grins like a Cheshire cat and purrs, "You have no idea."

* * *

Frankie

BENEDICT GOES STILL, and my smile falls away. "Benedict? Is something wrong?"

"No." He turns away and starts to pace in front of me. Once, twice. I don't think he realizes he's doing it. "Daniel says you're ready."

"Daniel's optimistic."

"No, he's not."

I shrug. Benedict keeps pacing. On the last pass, he turns to face me and holds out a small black velvet ring box.

My heart stutters to a stop.

"It's new," he says, as casually as if he bought me windshield wipers for my car. "I can't give you heirlooms."

"Of course not." This is all fake, after all. I take a deep breath and push down my disappointment. I have no right to be disappointed; I'm just the hired help. *I don't belong.*

But I'm still curious enough about what sort of ring he chose. "May I?"

At his nod, I open the little black box. The diamond flashes like starlight.

"Oh, you shouldn't have." My fingers tremble a little as I take the ring out. I don't know much about jewelry, and nothing about engagement rings, but this one is perfect. Classy. Not too ostentatious.

"Do you like it?" he asks, gruffly enough that I know my answer means something to him.

"I love it." I slip it on and hold up my hand to admire the sparkle. "It fits perfectly."

"Daniel was very thorough."

"Well." I drop my arm, suppressing a smile. "Aren't you going to ask me?"

He raises a brow. "Shall I get down on one knee?"

I can't help it. I burst out laughing.

"Miss Frankie, this is no laughing matter."

"I know. It's serious. It's just so… fake."

"I suppose we should do it correctly though." There's a gleam in his eye. He saunters towards me, six feet of handsome in Hugo Boss. My laughter drains away, leaving a quiver in its wake. The gaudy room with its ostentatious trappings falls away, along with the constant shrew-like voice telling me I don't belong. It's just us. Ordinary Frankie, and a movie-star handsome man who happens to be a duke.

"I suppose," I whisper.

He takes my hand, twisting the ring so it's settled on my finger. His touch lights sparklers in my bloodstream.

"Francis Beaumonde," if his deep voice didn't set off fire-works in my belly, the intensity in his coffee black eyes would, "Will you do me the honor of being my wife?"

"My goodness," I warble when I can speak. "You really sell it."

He says nothing, only strokes my fingers. I want to throw my arms around him, kiss him senseless, tell him yes. Instead, I muster up my sarcasm. "Oh wow, this is so unex-pected. Benedict, you shouldn't have. I'm the luckiest lady in the world." I hold out my hand, ignoring the slight softening of his normally severe mouth. "Seriously, Your Grace, you've outdone yourself."

He captures my hand again. "You were calling me Benedict."

"Not 'Your Highness'?" I snark back.

His fingers stroke my wrist. "I'm not a prince."

"Not yet. And you won't be without a Can Do Attitude." I use the most cheesy motivational speaker voice I can muster. "Think of me as your coach." I raise my hands like I have fake pom poms, and channel an obnoxious cheerleader. "Go team!"

"I'm going to regret this," Benedict mutters. He doesn't say it like he regrets it. He says it like he's consigned to his fate. Even bemused that he doesn't hate it.

"It's going to work out," I say more seriously. "Our engagement doesn't need to last long after Midsummer. We fake it until then, you get crowned, then you focus on your duty, and I sit at home and watch Elvis. A year later, we quietly break it off."

"Daniel coached you well."

"I'll stick to the contract."

"Mmm." He still hasn't let go of my hand, and it's getting distracting. "You'll have to spend time with me, of course.

Act like a fiancée. We can't sell it otherwise." His voice deepens. "Perhaps you should move in."

I swallow. "All right. As long as I can bring Elvis."

All softness drops from his expression. "I'll add an extra ten thousand ducats to the contract if you'll allow me to hire a sitter for him."

"But that's my job. Lady Drey hired me."

"And if you're too busy?"

"You're keeping me that busy?"

"I might need you at my side, morning, noon and night."

Oh my. "For what?" I fight to keep my voice nonchalant.

"Reasons."

"I don't know, dearest," I say sweetly. "The contract is temporary. You're going to have to learn to live without me."

"Tomorrow is important," he warns me softly. "If it doesn't go well, we need to call the whole thing off. And pray no one breaks the scandal."

"Why? What's tomorrow?"

"You meet one of my relatives. Lady Ursuline."

"She sounds like a bear."

His lips quirk but he doesn't rise to the bait. "She's my great aunt. The queen's mother's sister. Very important."

I swallow.

"Think of it as a practice session for meeting the queen."

"That important, huh?"

"Yes."

"All right. I'll do my best."

"You'll do fine, Frankie. Just remain fully clothed, and you'll be fine."

"You bastard." I swat his arm, laughing until I see his expression. "What is it?" I drop my hand. "What did I say?"

A slow breath out, and he visibly relaxes. "Nothing. It was nothing."

"Sorry. That was rude. I'm sorry."

"No, I…" He turns, and my breath catches at the sight of his beautiful profile. "It wasn't your fault. I overreacted."

"Daniel's making me memorize all sorts of protocol. Entries in *Kingman's Book of Peers*. But I think I'm better off keeping my mouth shut. I don't want to say the wrong thing, and ruin everything."

"You won't ruin everything."

"Do you really think so?" I whisper.

"You said it yourself: we're a team now. I won't let you fail." He offers me his arm and I take it. We're out of the room before I ask where we're going.

"Not far." He turns the corner, and I gasp. Set up in the middle of Lady Drey's room of antique horrors is a table for two—white tablecloth, fancy candelabra, the works. In the corner, Sir Fred stands guard, wearing a chef's hat atop his helmet.

"I asked Daniel if we could have dinner together. He thought it was a good idea." Benedict holds my chair and I sit carefully, praying I don't spill anything on my fancy ball gown.

Of course the first thing Benedict does is uncork and pour us wine.

"Oh, none for me," I protest as he fills my glass halfway.

"You must. You need to raise your tolerance. There will be plenty of wine and spirits at state dinners. It's the only way one gets through them."

I roll my eyes again, but successfully keep from telling him to fuck off. Progress.

Dinner is simple—fillet of fish, potatoes, and asparagus on a single plate, kept warm under a heavy silver dish cover. I pace myself and manage not to spill. The wine fills me with a warm glow, and with the candlelight flickering over Benedict's stunning if severe visage, I find myself enjoying myself.

After dinner, he leads me to yet another room—a study I

haven't been in before—and pours a brandy for himself, limoncello for me.

"What else is on Daniel's checklist?" he asks, lounging on the couch next to me.

"Uh, how to curtsey, when to curtsey, when to bow. The proper way to eat, drink, address an earl versus a queen."

"One doesn't address a queen. You sit and let her talk. My aunt won't bite."

"I hope not." I fake a laugh. "A biting monarch. That would be a headline."

"Speaking of which, there will be a few more of those. Headlines. We stopped the naked pictures from running, but Daniel had to promise an exclusive story about us. And pictures from the engagement photoshoot."

"We're doing a photoshoot?" I put a hand to my stomach.

"Unfortunately. We'll be the biggest news of the summer. Until the queen announces her pregnancy."

"And then names you official heir." I swirl the final bit of my limoncello and set the glass aside.

"Yes." Benedict downs the rest of his brandy. "I can't wait for it to be over."

I almost chime in, 'Me neither,' but it wouldn't be true. Because after this is over, there'll be no more Benedict. He'll be busy with affairs of state, and I'll be back to my reclusive life. He'll trot me out for a few ceremonies, and then we'll announce our breakup, and that will be it.

The clock in the corner ticks loudly, and I realize how long the silence has been.

"So…" I cast about for a neutral topic, one that won't start a fire. But my tongue gets the best of me. "Why aren't you married?"

"No time."

I bite my tongue. *Don't ask, don't ask, don't do it*—"You're not a virgin, are you?"

"No. Are you?"

"No." I wave my hand. "I've had boyfriends."

"Good." He sets his glass down and slides closer. Suddenly it is very, very warm in here. "You'll have had some practice."

"What?" I squeak.

"Kissing, Miss Beaumonde. Practice kissing." He's looking closely at my mouth.

Automatically, I lick my lips. "Should we practice?"

"Kissing?" He sounds thoughtful. "Not a bad idea. We are affianced."

I glance down at the ring. When I look up, his face is close to mine.

"Perhaps we should practice, just a little," I whisper.

He tips my face to his, fingers light on my jaw. Our lips meet, his close-clipped beard brushing my cheeks. A slow warmth spreads through my limbs, the sensation like the one I get after sipping brandy.

"Good girl," he whispers. "Now more."

I grab his lapels, surging up to rub my tender breasts against his firm chest. His tongue meets mine, stroke for stroke. It makes me wild. His body is rock steady under mine, controlled, and coiled tension tightly leashed. But his mouth speaks for itself, a language of passion and desire.

I'm shaking when I break away from him with a gasp. My body throbs, full of a delicious ache. I touch the skin around my lips, where it feels chafed from the scrape of his dark facial hair.

"There." He leans back. In the hazy light streaming from the lamps, he looks like a painting. *Portrait of a man satisfied.*

He pulls out his handkerchief, pats his lips. "That should mollify the papers."

My happy daze shatters. "What?"

"We'll do that every so often, when the photographers think we don't know they're watching." He tucks his handkerchief back into his breast pocket. I search his expression, but there's no sign he was affected at all by the kiss that made me reel. "Goodnight, Miss Beaumonde." With a cruel little twist to his lips, he gets up off the couch and stalks away, leaving me cold.

rankie

THE NEXT MORNING, I'm sitting in a sleek black limo, dressed in a navy skirt suit, trying not to hyperventilate. Daniel is watching me with concern.

"Breathe, Frankie. It'll go fine."

"I feel like I'm going to court." I raise my arms and look down at my Kate Middleton outfit. "I look like it, too."

"Lady Ursaline isn't going to cross-examine you. Well, she will, but you have nothing to fear."

"Oh god." I glance out the window as the limo rolls up to a monstrously large estate. The four-story stone front looks like something out of a Jane Austen movie set. Lady Drey's mansion could easily fit into one of the wings. *I feel faint.*

"Shall I fetch the smelling salts?" Daniel asks, and I realize I said what I was thinking out loud.

"Relax. Pay attention a minute." He taps his clipboard. "Did you and his Grace get your story straight? When you met, what you thought, how he fell for you? When he proposed?"

I nod. "We're sticking to the truth as much as possible. Except we'll say I was wearing clothes when I met him."

"No need to change that little detail." Daniel smirks. "It would explain love at first sight."

"I don't know if we can fake love."

"I think you'll do fine."

"It's not me I'm worried about," I mutter.

"Oh, I don't know. The duke is better at faking things than you might expect."

I frown, but Daniel doesn't explain. "Well, His Grace is making sure we rehearse everything. We even practiced kissing, so you can check that off your list."

Daniel blinks at me and then at his clipboard. "That wasn't on the list."

"Oh." My cheeks heat. "Extra credit then."

Daniel gives me a long look. "It's all an act, Frankie," he says finally. "All of this is fake."

"I know." I remember how the duke sauntered off after our kiss, totally unaffected. "I won't forget."

"If you say so."

The limo glides to a stop, and Daniel hops out to get my door. I twist and keep my knees together as I take his hand and exit the car.

And then Benedict is there, sauntering out of the grand home like he owns the place. Which he might, one day. He nods to Daniel and reaches out to greet me. "Darling, you look beautiful." He kisses my cheek.

I squeeze his hands like they're a lifeline. "Thank you, so do you." And he does, but he arches a brow at me. "Shut up," I whisper. "I'm nervous."

"Relax. She'll like you." He offers his arm and I take it.

"Daniel says she'll give me the third degree."

"Yes, but she only does that with people she likes."

"Oh well, that's all right then." I gulp down air as we stroll casually through a home so grand, it should be a museum. It *is* a museum—of giant classical landscape paintings and Baroque architecture.

"Did Daniel tell you the schedule for the day?" Benedict asks as we come to a door guarded by two footmen. He nods to them, and they sweep the doors open for us to walk through. This room is a bit smaller than the rest we've passed through—meaning you can't fit my childhood home in it, just the first floor. There's a long table adorned with cornucopias overflowing with grapes. All this pomp and ceremony for *brunch*.

"Um, he did but I didn't catch all of it." I was too busy trying not to hyperventilate. Like now.

Benedict brings me to a chair and pulls it out for me to sit. "After this, we'll go to the courthouse to post banns. There's a little ceremony we'll attend after, nothing taxing. Tomorrow a press conference to announce the engagement, then a party for a visiting diplomat. And Friday is a ball."

"Fun." I feel sick. "I've never been to a ball."

"We'll dance. Drink. Then fireworks."

I force a smile. "I'm always down for fireworks."

Benedict seats himself next to me. There are twenty chairs on our side of the table alone, and I have no idea why.

"Are we expecting company?" I motion to the seats.

"No, just Lady Ursuline. She likes to take breakfast in the lesser dining hall."

"Of course. Very bourgeois. I'd do the same." There are three forks beside my plate. I touch them, trying to remember what they're for. Salad, main course, and… I can't remember what the extra one does. Oh well, I can use it to kill myself if I make a mistake.

"Frankie." Benedict takes my hand and peels my fingers

away from the item of silverware. He sets the fork in its proper place and closes his large hands over mine. "Relax."

"I am relaxed. I am. Did you know the 1812 Overture wasn't written by Tchaikovsky to commemorate the War of 1812? I didn't know that. Americans play it on the Fourth of July, along with their fireworks. But it's not about America. It's about Russia defeating Napoleon." I inhale a deep breath.

Benedict blinks slowly. "I think I did know that, actually."

"Okay. Okay. Good." I bob my head up and down. "I talk when I'm nervous."

"I hadn't noticed." His deep voice soothes me, while his fingers stroke the inside of my wrist. "It's all right."

"And if it's not?"

"Then I'll consider ways to keep you quiet." The look he gives me is pure heat. He raises my hand to his lips and kisses it, looking like a man in love.

He's not. He's not in love. It's fake, fake, fake. Fake it, Frankie.

I let my face melt into an adoring simper. Benedict's dark eyes widen slightly, then the corners crinkle. "That's the spirit."

* * *

BENEDICT

FRANKIE GAZES UP AT ME, the portrait of a woman in love. Then she flutters her eyelashes at me.

"Now that's overkill." I rise and replace my chair, heading to my proper place on the other side of the table.

Frankie fidgets with her fork again, but she's lost the panicked look she had before.

I signal the footmen to enter. They serve coffee and, after a few sips, she regains the color in her cheeks.

"Better?" I ask.

"Much." She smacks her lips, but it's too adorable for me to chastise her for it. I've never seen anyone enjoy a cup of coffee so much. "You know," she says, looking around thoughtfully. "The table decorations match the paintings."

"You noticed." I grimace at the huge still-lifes surrounding us. "Well done."

She sits back, frowning. "Be nice to me."

"Or else?"

"Or else," she lowers her voice, "I'll put itching powder in your suit."

The corner of my mouth jerks up. I force it back down. "You would not."

She raises her brows. "Try me, Your Grace."

I'm contemplating what I can threaten her with when my great aunt bustles in. "Benny, darling," she booms.

I rise and bow. "Aunt Ursaline."

"Oh, sit, sit." My aunt settles into her chair at the head of the table and leans back to let the footman place her napkin in her lap. She frowns at Frankie. "And you're Miss Francis."

"My lady." Frankie has also risen to curtsey. I nod approval and motion for her to wait for the footman to pull out her chair.

"American?" My aunt looks down her nose at her plate. "I don't approve of Americans. Too much brash and bluster."

Frankie wears an angelic expression rarely seen outside of paintings of the Madonna. It makes me nervous. "I understand. But better to be loud than demure and unheard."

Auntie Ursaline harrumphs. "Well said. Where'd you find her, Benny?"

Frankie shoots me a look and mouths, *Benny?*

I shake my head slightly and reach across the table for Frankie's hand. It's small and light. For all her 'brash and bluster', she's rather dainty. "We happen to be neighbors," I say. "We met when her parrot escaped—"

"He's not my parrot," Frankie interrupts, and flushes when she realizes what she's done. "I mean, excuse me. But I don't own the parrot or the house. I'm just pet sitting."

"Pet sitting? Exactly what does that entail?" My aunt sets about fixing her tea, adding milk, two lumps of sugar, and giving it precisely two stirs before draining the whole cup. Frankie watches closely.

"Well, I find pets… and I sit on them."

"What?" My aunt sets the cup down with a clatter. I squeeze Frankie's fingers.

"I care for them, my lady," Frankie corrects.

"Hmmm." My aunt is not fooled. "And does one make a living at this?"

"One does. I started when I was fifteen, and got really good at it. Uh, I tend to throw in extra services—an hour a day walking or playing with their pet—for free. I also make homemade treats. The dogs love them. And…" She hesitates, as if realizing how passionate she sounds. But even my aunt can't resist her enthusiasm.

"Go on," Lady Ursaline says.

"So, my most inspired moment was writing a funny little postcard from a Shih Tzu to her 'mommy'. I even got the dog to stamp her foot in ink and 'sign' the card. The owner loved it, raved about me to her friends, and I started getting bigger and better jobs offered by people who wanted more of an animal nanny."

"Fascinating. I have a few friends who would love to use you. Of course, as a duchess, you'll hardly have time for this *pet sitting.*"

"Of course." Frankie lowers her eyes and prepares her tea exactly as my aunt did. She looks pretty and demure, but I'm not fooled. Half of me wants to have her argue with my aunt, just so I can hear what she might say.

"I'll want Frankie to pursue her own career and interests, of course," I say. "As I do."

"You'll have little time for your own pet projects, Benedict. With the duties of state, combined with the role of President, you'll have to give up your position at the Ministry of Finance."

I hardly hear my aunt, because Frankie is choking on her tea. I thump her back and offer a handkerchief.

"Miss Beaumonde, are you all right?"

"I beg your pardon, my lady. I swallowed wrong." She wipes her streaming eyes. When she goes to return the handkerchief, she grabs my hand. "President?" she whispers.

"What are you two carrying on about? Youngsters these days. Always muttering. Not good for the lungs. Sit up straight and let your voice carry." My aunt demonstrates, bellowing the last part.

"Forgive me, my lady," I say. "Frankie was merely inquiring about the presidential role."

"Ah yes, President. It'll be good for the country to have a proper one again," Lady Ursaline says. "About time you took your rightful place, Benny dear."

"Wait, is this for real? You're going to be President?" Frankie looks aghast.

"It's more of a ceremonial role," I hasten to explain. "The President is elected by both popular and electoral vote, but a Crown Prince or Princess most often holds the role."

"You have a queen, a parliament, a president, and a prime minister?" Frankie asks. "Isn't that overkill?"

"Impertinent girl," Lady Ursaline says, almost fondly. "New Arcadia has existed for a millennium. We have perfected our government. Your country is a young upstart compared with our history."

"But isn't this New Arcadia? What happened to Old Arcadia?"

"What do you mean?" My aunt is suddenly busy eating her eggs.

"Well, America has New York. New Jersey. There's New Zealand. But this is New Arcadia. What happened to the old one?" Frankie's eyes are very wide in an expression of innocence. "Did you lose it?"

"Such insolence," my aunt exclaims in a way that tells me she's having more fun than she's had in years. "We lost nothing. As it happens, this country was founded by former knights of the round table. Brave fellows, but they knew nothing of finance. The kingdom almost fell into ruin before King Otto Reupprecht the Wise invented the pretzel."

"Invented the pretzel?" Frankie wrinkles her nose.

"He did. The financial success saved our nation. And he renamed the country New Arcadia to celebrate its rebirth."

"I guess that makes sense," Frankie says slowly.

"Of course it does. It's our history! Makes perfect sense." Lady Ursaline thumps the table so hard, the dishes rattle. "King Otto was Benedict's ancestor, you know. Genius financial brain on that one."

"And what did you invent, Your Grace?" Frankie turns to me, feigning more wide-eyed innocence that means she's trying to stir up trouble. "The croissant?"

"No. A system of taxation that feeds a citizens' trust and provides a demogrant."

"Right." Frankie spears a piece of sausage before informing me, "I understand precisely none of that."

"Genius," Lady Ursaline crows, patting her mouth and waving the footman over to order more stewed tomatoes.

"It's a citizens' dividend," I explain. "Universal basic income."

"You have that?" Frankie looks impressed.

"Yes."

"And Benedict came up with it all," Lady Ursaline says.

Frankie seems truly curious when she asks, "How did you do it?"

I focus on my plate, which is rude, but Frankie's attention is rather flattering. Typically, when I bring up economics with a brunch date, their eyes glaze over. Which is probably why Frankie is my first date in five years. "It's made possible by a specific tax on the nation's highest dividend earners."

"It mostly affects members of the royal family," Lady Ursaline says, waving her cloth napkin before patting her lips. "A tax on the royal fund. Didn't they moan and groan over that one?" She looks absolutely delighted at the thought of a bevy of complaining royals. "Made him quite unpopular with our set."

That's an understatement. The tax bill wasn't expected to pass, but when it did, officials took notice. Overnight, I made enemies—many of them members of my own family. Which makes holiday dinners quite uncomfortable. Not that socializing with my own set was ever very enjoyable.

"Let me get this straight." Frankie sets down her fork and leans closer to me, her cheeks flushed in that charming way they get when she's excited. "You implemented a tax on dividends that pays into a fund. And you take the dividends on that and give money to everyone in the country."

"That's right," Lady Ursaline says, "Everyone, from the eldest citizen to the smallest child."

"The royal fund is in the trillions. We can well afford it. It was the right thing to do," I tell Frankie quietly.

She's looking at me as if she's seeing me anew. "That's incredible."

I shake my head slightly. "Anyone would have done it."

"They didn't. You did." She goes back to eating, a small smile on her face. "You should be proud."

And, for the first time since implementing the tax and fighting it through to law, I am.

* * *

Frankie

DANIEL IS WAITING for us when we leave Lady Ursaline's palatial home. "Well?"

"It didn't go so badly," I report.

"No?" Daniel looks to the duke to confirm. Benedict raises his chin slightly. "Good then. We'll debrief later."

"Frankie, ride with me," Benedict orders. He helps me into the car and waits until the divider goes up between us and the driver before turning to me. "You are entirely too naughty, Miss Beaumonde."

"Really, Benny?" I slouch in the seat. It feels good to lounge and indulge in manspread.

"Don't call me that."

"Or else what?"

"I'll punish you."

I ignore the warning signal flashing: *Danger! Danger!* "How do you propose to do that? Force me to actually marry you?"

"That's it," he growls, and pounces.

I end up on my back with one hundred and eighty pounds of lean strength on top of me. The duke catches my wrists easily and pins them above my head.

"Now I've got you."

"So you do. Now what?"

"Find a way to shut that mouth." He lowers his head and kisses me. Sensation sizzles through me. My toes curl so hard, my heels fall off. My feet scrabble on the seat, trying for lever-age. I want to press my hips into his, press my whole body against his firm one. Benedict stops my struggles, pinning me soundly. He reaffirms his grip on my wrists and I can't even slide my fingers into his silky hair. My fingers flex, palms itching to touch him. I whimper and he draws back to give me a dark smile, enjoying my helplessness before his lips stroke at mine again. His tongue invades my mouth, licking the insides of my cheeks until I'm rocking under him, unable to do anything but spar with his tongue with little licks of my own.

When he finally draws back, I'm a puddle of goo on the car seat. Woozy as if I've drunk a draught of brandy.

"Fuck, Benedict," I pant. Vaguely, I sense him with-drawing further, a huge dark hunger camouflaged in a civi-lized suit. "Fuck me." I reach for him but he's already sliding away.

"Not here, darling. We're at the courthouse." He straightens his already perfectly straight tie, and flicks a glance over me. "Fix your hair."

He exits the car, leaving me to pull the scattered pieces of myself together. Daniel's waiting on the curb, folio in hand. The two bend their heads close. Benedict looks as cool and crisp as ever. His hair and suit are unrumpled. Meanwhile, I look like I've been tossed in a dryer.

"Fuck you, Benedict," I mutter, combing my fingers through my hair. Damn him for making a game out of seducing me. Testing his control and mocking mine.

No more. I'm never kissing him again.

I bundle my hair into a bun, smooth my skirt and find my shoes. My lips are still puffy. I swing out of the car, and before my heels have hit the sidewalk, Benedict's attention snaps to me. My lips first, and then my cleavage. And as I sway towards him, I get an idea.

I will kiss him again. But this time, I'll win. Leave him wrecked instead of me.

I'll be the best damn fake fiancée he could ask for. I'll act so well, I'll win a damn Emmy. And I'll make him sorry he ever toyed with me.

I slow my walk the final few steps, and savor the way the conversation between Daniel and the duke drops away.

"Ready, Miss Beaumonde?" Benedict offers his arm.

Oh yes. I sidle up to him and take it, leaning close enough to brush my breasts against his bicep. Then I look up at him through my lashes, noting the slight widening of his pupils. His gaze goes unfocused a moment. "Ready, darling," I murmur.

This is war.

* * *

Frankie

"He kissed you?" Mina gasps into her headset microphone later that night. "For reals?"

"For reals reals," I confirm. I'm in the movie room with Elvis. *To Catch a Thief* is playing on the screen, but I'm too wound up to watch.

"Was it good?"

"It was incredible."

"Aww, yeah." Mina types faster. "And I called it."

On screen, Cary Grant gives Grace Kelly some side eye as she lead-foots the convertible up the mountain. "It doesn't mean anything. It was just a kiss."

"A good kiss isn't nothing." Her typing hits hyperdrive. Any faster, and her keyboard will catch fire. "So things are moving along?"

"We posted the banns, whatever that means. After that, we attended a small ceremony—the christening of a new building for the Ministry of Finance. Benedict cut the ribbon. The press got wind of our engagement, but didn't arrive until we were about to leave."

"I saw it. He does look good in a suit."

"Yeah," I reluctantly agree. I've got to up my game if I'm going to hold up my end of the bargain. I need to be more like Grace Kelly. Demure, elegant, less of a mess. "We have a bunch more little ceremonies to attend this week. Daniel thinks it's good for us to be seen together this way."

"Kind of boring." Mina hates sitting still for longer than two minutes—but she's fine with sitting and typing for hours on end. "Bring a book."

"Ha." Both Daniel and the duke would give me the evil eye if I pulled out a copy of *War and Peace* during a royal function. "New Arcadia loves their ceremonies. Get this, once Benedict is Crown Prince, he'll probably also be elected President. It's a ceremonial role."

"Oh, like Iceland. Iceland has a set up like that. Look it up."

"I will." I take a moment to pause the movie before the scene with the fireworks kiss. I love a good fireworks kiss. "You know, it's kinda weird Benedict hasn't been officially crowned prince before now. He's heir presumptive."

"Is he now?" Mina's back to banging on her keyboard. Sometimes I think she plays video games while we talk. "Well, la dee da."

"Benedict already does a lot of what a President would do. Ribbon cutting, flag raising, that sort of thing."

"Well, today his flag was raised, all right. Or should I say, flagpole."

"Mina!"

She snickers. "Lucky you."

"For the last time: I'm not sleeping with him."

"Your loss. I'd never pass up a chance to get some good dick. *Bene* dick, get it?"

"Goodbye, Mina." I close my laptop. "Is it even possible?" I wonder aloud to Elvis. He shakes his feathers. "Me and the duke. The duke and me. I. Whatever."

Elvis waits patiently for me to figure out my grammar.

"It's stupid." I bite my lip. I've never told anyone the full story.

What the hell, I'm talking to a parrot.

"I once knew a girl who dallied with a rich boy. They fooled around. Always in secret. And then she missed her period." Elvis cocks his grey head to the side like he's listening. "I wish I could tell you the story had a happy ending." I smile sadly. "But real life isn't a fairytale."

I need to remember that.

rankie

OUR FIRST PRESS conference as a couple is held outside, in a park near the queen's palace. Daniel's set us up at a long table in front of rows and rows of flowers. A few hundred feet to the right is a famous fountain crowned with a giant statue of a pretzel. I always wondered about the pretzel. Thanks to Lady Ursaline, I now know why New Arcadia has so many pretzel statues.

Benedict takes point, thanking the press for coming. I sit up straight and channel Grace Kelly as he outlines the vigors of his career and state responsibilities, how he's wished for a family but been too busy for social concerns, etc., etc. The speech is all very pretty and a bit self-deprecating, but Benedict pulls it off with gravitas.

"And so I'm pleased to announce my engagement to Francis Beaumonde, of the Grant County Beaumondes."

My smile turns a bit brittle. No way this story isn't

getting out into the world, and back to my hometown. The Grant County Beaumondes, indeed. I can't imagine what my Grandmère will think of all this. Not that I'll ever know.

"Please treat her with respect, and give her the Arcadian welcome she deserves."

I rise and come to Benedict's side. He puts his arm around me. Cameras flash, and I smile into them as gracefully as I can.

"Your Grace! Your Grace!" Reporters raise their hands.

Daniel rushes to take Benedict's place at the microphone. "No questions at this time. His Grace is a very busy man…"

"Well done," Benedict whispers in my ear, steering me away. Bodyguards fall into step, keeping the press at bay.

"What now?" There's an intensity to his voice that makes me think all is not so calm under the surface.

"Act like you're in love," he orders. "At this very moment, the press is researching your name. They're going to find out you're a commoner. Not only that, you're American."

I tilt my head at him and laugh softly. "Oh Benny. You say the sweetest things."

"Just telling the truth. And don't call me Benny."

I narrow my eyes at him before I remember I'm supposed to look like I'm in love with the twit.

"Come," he says, glancing over his shoulder and tugging me down a garden path.

"Are we in a hurry?"

"Yes." He makes no more effort to explain. I search for a more neutral topic before I explode.

"Oh, look at that," I say as we pass an outdoor stage. "It's perfect for a concert. Or a play. You could even get a projector and host old movies after dark, whenever it's warm."

Benedict sniffs. There are a few shouts behind us, too

distant for me to hear what they're saying. Our guards have fallen away.

"Surely there's enough money in the trillion dollar budget," I pant. Benedict's strides are so long, I have to trot to keep up.

"The royal fund is at a trillion dollars, not our budget." We round a hedge and exit the garden.

I'm jogging now. "Still, it would be a nice public program."

"Those sorts of pet projects aren't my jurisdiction. Come along." Benedict makes a beeline towards our waiting limo.

"Jerkhole," I mutter. But when we're safely ensconced in our ride, I notice his eyes are a bit wild.

"To the embassy," he orders the driver. As we pull away from the curb, he whips out a handkerchief and wipes his brow.

"Are you all right?" I ask. I've never seen him sweat. Up until now, I didn't think dukes were capable of basic bodily functions.

"Fine." He spares me a short glance. "I hate press conferences."

"I guess you'll have to do a lot of them, when you're crowned prince."

"Unfortunately."

The limo turns a corner, and I see our guards. They're holding back a mass of reporters.

"Filthy fucking vultures," Benedict mutters. "Forgive me."

"It's fine. You sure you're all right? We could skip our next event, just go home."

"And risk Daniel's wrath?" He wipes his forehead one more time before stuffing the white square of fabric back into his pocket. "No hiding at home, Miss Beaumonde. That's not a luxury I have."

And the arrogant duke is back, before I even had a chance

to miss him. "You know, if you get nervous, you could use that old actor trick. Imagine everyone in their underwear. Or naked."

"I doubt that will help. And I don't have that much imagination, thank god. Of course…" He slides closer as the car glides up to our next stop. My chest is heaving from our rush, but he looks as perfect as ever.

He puts his hand on the door handle then leans in the opposite direction—towards me. "Of course, if I thought of you, I wouldn't have to imagine." And he gives me a look that sets off fireworks in the pit of my belly before turning to exit the car.

And that, ladies and gentlemen, is how you distract a duke.

* * *

Frankie

"Well done!" Daniel greets us just inside the door and waves us into a private office. "It went splendidly. And now for your first party. Are you ready, Frankie?"

"Of course." After a few false starts, I give him what I hope is a reassuring smile. I'm still a little worried about Benedict. He looms at my side, stone-faced and brooding.

"You'll do beautifully. And Lady Ursaline will vouch for you."

"She's here?" I ask, just as her voice booms in the foyer. "Good. I like her."

"She approves of you." Daniel opens the door a crack and peeks out. "All right, duckies. Into the fray."

"Remember: underwear," I whisper to Benedict as he escorts me out. His lips twitch. Win.

Me, I've decided to play Katherine Hepburn tonight. A shorter, curvier version.

Daniel tugs me aside for a debrief after a half hour, under the pretext of handing me some champagne. "How are you doing?"

"I'm good. Lady Ursaline's helping." I sip the bubbly drink as fast as I can. Hobnobbing makes me super thirsty.

"Excellent. I knew the old dragon would come through."

"How come she gets to say whatever she wants, and I don't?"

Daniel shrugs. "Benefit of being a peer. When you're born into five generations of royalty, you can do what you want."

"Doesn't seem fair."

"You're doing fine." He captures the champagne glass before I can guzzle the rest. "But I do have a bit of advice."

I sigh. "Yes?"

"Tone down the accent."

"Whenever I talk to people, I pretend I'm Katherine Hepburn," I admit. "Too weird?"

"Yes. Please stop. And don't tell anyone that." He pulls out his phone and checks it. "Your name is trending in the news."

"Great."

"It was bound to happen. It's mostly positive or neutral. Just keep doing what you're doing. Except," he holds up a finger, "less Katherine, and more Audrey."

For the rest of the night, I channel soft-spoken ingenue. It works marvelously.

I also ignore Benedict. Not obviously. But as soon as he joins a conversation, I find a reason to move on. I follow Lady Ursaline, and she's only too happy to introduce me to everyone she knows. It doesn't take long for Benedict to catch on. I sense his frustration when I give him the slip for the third time. He stalks me slowly, back and forth across the room. The hair on the back of my neck stands up in warning. I'm being hunted. When his presence is a ball of brooding tension, a duke-shaped nuclear reactor ready to explode, I excuse myself a final time and slip into a side room for a breather. A minute later, Benedict's footsteps follow.

"Miss Beaumonde."

"Why, hello, Your Grace. Fancy meeting you here."

He strolls right up, parks himself close. "I'm imagining you naked. Why do you think that is?"

"You have an active imagination?"

"I'm sure that's not it." He teases a stray strand of my hair back from my face. I hold my breath as his finger traces my ear, down my neck, and starts to play with the strap on my shoulder.

My thoughts escape me, slippery as fish. "Perhaps," I half gasp, "it's the same reason I've been imagining you naked all night."

His finger drifts along my collarbone. "You are entirely naughty."

"Or imaginative." I turn slowly and put my back to him, pretending to study the artwork on the wall.

"I should teach you a lesson," he growls, coming up behind me. Despite myself, my heart jumps.

I press my behind into him. Mina's right—he has a very impressive flagpole. "Don't make promises you don't intend to keep."

He draws me close and escorts me to the next room, where he whirls me around.

"Careful, Benny *dear*," I mimic Lady Ursaline's accent. "You'll rumple my dress."

"Don't call me that." His hands close on my shoulders. "You're ignoring me. I'd like to know why."

"No reason." I give him a saccharine smile. "Sugar plum."

"No."

"Sweetie pie."

"I think not."

"Tickly-poo. Babycakes."

His dark eyes flash. "You're dangerously close to crossing a line, Miss Beaumonde. Choose your next words wisely."

I think a moment, then lean close, holding his eyes. "Pookie." Our mouths are so close, I can feel his breath puff against my lips.

"That's it," He hauls me against him. I stifle my glee, but can't help grinning like a fool. "You, me, tonight. You're getting what you deserve."

"Oh yeah? What's that, Your Grace?" I lift my arms and cross them behind his neck.

"Ahem, lovebirds," Daniel trills, wafting through the room. "Not too much alone time this soon. People will talk."

Benedict draws back, but not before I run my nails up the back of his neck, ruffling his hair.

"Next time," he promises darkly, and stalks after Daniel. The duke's tie is askew, and a few tufts of hair are sticking up in the back. Not much, but it's a start.

A half hour later, Lady Ursaline is introducing me to another boring diplomat when a prickle on the back of my neck tells me someone is looming behind me. I turn, and there's Benedict.

He takes my hand. "Darling, I simply must steal you away."

"Of course, honey bun. If y'all will excuse me," I singsong to the guests who are now smiling behind their champagne at our ridiculous romance.

"You are incorrigible," Benedict says, sweeping me into a waltz.

"Not true. I'm entirely corrigible. One hundred percent." I sigh like a woman basking in the arms of her love.

"Daniel thinks you're acting strangely."

"I'm not acting strangely. I'm acting like Audrey Hepburn," I tell him. "Earlier, I was channeling Katherine. And before that, at the press conference, I was Grace Kelly."

"I see."

"It's all an act." I keep my voice down. "And we're both in on it. You make an excellent Cary Grant."

"Thank you," he says gravely. Exactly like Cary Grant would answer if you gave him a compliment.

The music changes and our steps slow.

After a while, I muse, mostly to myself, "Why would I be Frankie, when I could be someone more glamorous?"

"I don't know," he sounds equally thoughtful, "I've grown fond of the original Frankie. Although," his voice deepens, "she is quite naughty."

"I'm sure I have no idea what you mean," I say in a very proper tone.

He waltzes me to a corner, where he presses me close with a firm hand on the small of my back. His lips find my ear. "I'm serious. You're getting what you deserve. Tonight."

"You never did tell me what exactly I deserve."

"A lesson in manners."

"Can't. I'm teaching Elvis to rap. I'll be up all night." I arch backwards, exaggerating my posture as we turn together so each move 'accidentally' rubs my breasts against his chest.

Benedict's eyes narrow as he studies me. "*You're a rare parrot teacher.*"

I recognize the quote from *Much Ado About Nothing*. "*A bird of my tongue is better than a beast of yours,*" I deliver the next line with a grin.

"*I would my horse had the speed of your tongue,*" he says, and then adds, "My naughty lady Beatrice."

The quartet plays the final measures of the waltz and we break apart. He bows and I curtsey. When I rise, I tell him, "That's not the next line, you know."

"Oh?" He offers his arm. "Perhaps you should tutor me later. In private."

"Perhaps, Your Grace. If I'm not teaching my parrot." Pretending not to see his proffered arm, I drift away.

Daniel swoops in before I get very far across the room. "Champagne, Miss Beaumonde?" he asks loudly, and escorts me to the bar. "What is going on between you two?" he hisses in my ear.

"Nothing." I accept a champagne flute.

"It's not nothing. The tension is palpable." He fans his face with a hand. "But you've led him on a merry chase all night."

Across the room, Benedict takes his place in a circle of people surrounding his aunt. But his gaze is fixed on me.

"I'm not the sort of woman to hang all over a man," I say, slipping back into a Katherine Hepburn accent. "I find it gauche."

"Frankie," Daniel casts a worried look at the duke, "I don't know what game you two are playing…"

"It's not a game." I sip my champagne.

"Friday's your first ball. It needs to go perfectly."

"And it will. It's fine, Daniel." I raise my glass to Benedict in a silent toast before turning my back on him. "Just a bit of theater."

And may the best actress win.

* * *

BENEDICT

MY FIANCÉE IS TRYING to drive me mad. It's the only explanation for her behavior. In public, we flirt and cling to each other like the lovers we're pretending to be. In private, she keeps me coolly at arm's length. No more trysts in the limo. No more sparring while we waltz. She's entirely buttoned up, playing the role of my fiancée with not a hint of the clever, clumsy Frankie.

Daniel is in raptures over how well things are going. The officials we've met are charmed by Frankie, or won over by Lady Ursaline's opinion. Even the press are coming around.

I hate it. I want the old Frankie back. And I will do anything to get her.

The night of our first ball, I find myself back in Lady Drey's home. Frankie is upstairs dressing while I wait at the bottom of the stairs.

Daniel finds me there, pacing. "Trouble in paradise?"

"No. No trouble. Are they almost done?"

"Can't rush perfection," Daniel says lightly.

"I beg your pardon." I brush at my forehead. "It's been a long week."

"You and Frankie have done well. The press is satisfied. The public loves her."

I snort. "They adore her. She's way more popular than I am."

"Your tendency to speak only about fiscal policy is off putting. Frankie is charming. And her idea about summertime movies and concerts in the park would be very popular with the people."

"As long as it's not Shakespeare," I mutter, and check the time. "Should we fetch her? The ball is starting."

"A lady is never late," Daniel says. "But neither is she early, if she wishes to be fashionable."

My lip curls. "And I care so much for fashion."

"You should." Daniel jerks his chin upwards. "When that is the result."

Frankie's standing at the top of the stairs. Her hair is down and her shoulders are bare, but her arms are covered by long white gloves. Pure sin, those gloves. I'd get her in private, remove everything but the gloves, and have her stroke me...

I clench my fists, willing my body back under control. "Purple," I murmur.

"The color of royalty," Daniel murmurs back.

Frankie descends with regal slowness and glides across the floor, wearing a little Mona Lisa smile.

When she reaches us, she spreads her skirts in a slow curtsey. Automatically, Daniel and I bow.

"Your Grace." She sways towards me. Even her voice is throaty, dreamy.

"Miss Beaumonde." I offer my arm. "Shall we?"

I can't take my eyes off her. Not in the car, not when we arrive. And Frankie pretends to ignore me the whole time.

"Nervous?" I ask as we walk the press gauntlet together, and join the line to enter the residence.

"Not at all. Should I be?"

"I suppose you're old hat at these sorts of events. Especially after the Carrot Competition."

"Pageant. And that's fighting dirty, darling." She looks impressed. "You've been studying Daniel's notes about me."

"I need all the ammunition I can get."

"Are we fighting, Your Grace?"

"It feels like it." A few reporters are shouting at both of us. I put my arm around Frankie, shielding her from the fray.

"All couples have their spats, I suppose. All part of the drama." She leans past me and blows a kiss to the crowd. When they cheer, calling her name, she waves like a queen.

"You're becoming quite the method actress, Miss Beaumonde."

"Oh, I don't know." She lets me steer her inside. "Not all of it is an act."

But a slight tremor runs through her when we enter the ballroom. Frankie gauges the landscape like a mountaineer her ascent. Or descent, as it were. Our first hurdle is a grand staircase. Frankie pauses at the top for barely a second before trying to plunge forward.

"Wait." I hold her back with slight pressure on her glove-clad arm. "We wait for them to announce us." I nod to the herald standing in full regalia on the top step. He nods back, and takes a deep breath.

"HIS GRACE THE DUKE OF NEW ARCADIA, BENE-DICT FREDERICK LEOPOLD ALBERT OTTO REUP-PRECHT MONTEBATTEN—" the herald shouts in one breath.

"My goodness," Frankie says. "That's a lot of names." She starts to step forward and I hold her back, clamping her arm tighter.

"He's not done," I murmur.

"FERDINAND CHRISTIAN-LUDWIG VON CLEMENS-BILGESIRE—" The herald pauses to draw breath. Frankie looks to me, wide-eyed. I shake my head.

"—EARL OF CHIPPOWENTH, BARON REGIN, ROYAL KNIGHT OF THE MOST NOBLE ORDER OF THE GARTER, EXTRA KNIGHT OF THE MOST ANCIENT AND MOST NOBLE ORDER OF THE POPPYSEED, MEMBER OF THE ORDER OF THE MERITORIOUS PRETZEL, ROYAL CHIEF OF THE ORDER OF BUGA-BOO, EXTRAORDINARY COMPANION OF THE ORDER OF THE HONEY BADGER…"

"These can't all be real. He's making stuff up," Frankie whispers.

"Hush," I whisper back and fight a smile.

"EXTRAORDINARY COMMANDER OF THE ORDER OF MILITARY MERIT, LORD OF HER MAJESTY'S MOST HONOURABLE PRIVY COUNCIL, PRIVY COUNCILLOR OF THE QUEEN'S PRIVY COUNCIL FOR LYONNESSE—"

"I thought a privy was a toilet," Frankie mutters.

"LORD HIGH ADMIRAL—"

"Admiral?" Frankie asks. "Isn't New Arcadia landlocked?"

"We have a river. Shhh."

"PERSONAL AIDE-DE-CAMP TO HER MAJESTY, GRAND MASTER AND FIRST AND PRINCIPAL KNIGHT GRAND CROSS OF THE MOST EXCELLENT ORDER OF LYONNESSE, KNIGHT OF THE ORDER OF NEW ARCA-DIA, ADDITIONAL MEMBER OF THE ORDER OF FINANCE, EXTRA COMPANION OF THE QUEEN'S SERVICE ORDER..."

"Almost there," I murmur.

"AND..." The herald looks down at the podium, checking his notes.

"This is you," I tell Frankie. "Wait for it."

"AND GUEST."

I sweep down the stairs, drawing Frankie along. All around the room, people turn to stare at us. Whispers spread in ripples around the room, louder than the live orchestra.

"And guest?" Frankie hisses as I pull her into my arms and swing us into step with the other dancers. "That's it? You get all those titles, and I'm *and guest*?"

"If you marry me, you'll have plenty of titles of your own."

"No, thank you." She follows my lead perfectly and we execute tight circles, spinning around the room. "I don't want to have to wait for someone to list all my titles before I can enter a room. What if I have to pee?"

"You wouldn't always have to wait for a herald to announce all your titles. Just when you come to a ball."

"Never go to a ball again. No loss there."

"Oh, come off it, Miss Beaumonde. Don't tell me you're not having fun."

"Okay. I won't tell you." She smirks to herself. So fucking adorable. I spin her out and guide her into a series of promenade steps. It's either that or kiss her right here, right now.

We complete two turns of the room before I gather her back into my arms.

"I am, actually," she admits. "Having fun. I never thought I'd have fun in a nice dress and heels. I've had some traumatic experiences in them."

"Ah yes, the infamous Miss Carrot Competition."

"Beauty Pageant."

"The judges were fools if they didn't crown you the winner."

"What makes you say that?"

"You were the most beautiful girl in the county."

She snorts. "You don't know that."

"I do. Don't cross me, Miss Beaumonde," I order, and her lip curls as it always does when I say something arrogant. "I know because you're easily the most beautiful woman in this room. In fact, you're the most beautiful woman I've ever met."

She catches her breath. "Thank you," she says.

"For the compliment, or the dance?" I ask.

She shakes her head. Before she can retort, my aunt pushes between us.

"There you are, Benny dear," she bellows loudly enough, couples all around us turn to see what's causing the commotion. "About time you stopped hogging Miss Beaumonde. I'd like to introduce her to my set. Come along." Lady Ursaline bustles off, with us in tow.

"I still don't understand why Lady Ursaline gets to say whatever she wants, and I can't," Frankie says.

"You're young and conforming to the set." I place an extra hand over hers as I guide her through the parting sea of partygoers. Most stop and stare at Frankie, though she doesn't seem to notice. "Lady Ursaline's a dowager. Dowagers say whatever they please."

"How do I get to be a dowager?"

"Marry a duke and outlive him."

"Tempting," Frankie pronounces, and I chuckle, just as my great aunt stops.

"Why, Benedict," my aunt peers through her spectacles, "are you smiling?"

I immediately school my features into a more proper expression.

"Too late, I already saw it," my aunt trumpets. "Well done, Miss Beaumonde."

"Thank you, my lady," Frankie says automatically. "May I ask what I've done?"

"You're good for him," Lady Ursaline pronounces.

Frankie blinks.

"Come, let me introduce you to my set. Not all of them are boring." She sails off, leaving us to follow in her wake. Most people scatter out of her path, but an elderly gentleman in military dress doesn't realize he's been set upon before too late. "Ahhh, Colonel. Good to see you."

"Lady Ursaline, charmed." The colonel squints at us. Deaf and half blind, if I remember correctly.

"You know my great nephew, the duke." My aunt gestures to me, and I bow. "And this is his fiancée. An American."

"Ah, very good." The colonel peers at Frankie. "And who are you, my dear?"

"And guest," Frankie quips with a curtsey.

"Eh?" The colonel cocks an ear. "What's that, young lady? Ann Guest?"

"It's Ann Guest," his wife shouts in his ear.

"Christ," I mutter and dip to drop a warning in my naughty fiancée's ear. "Behave."

Frankie just smiles. It's all I can do not to haul her off into the corner and claim her mouth.

"Excuse us." I cut our exchange mercifully short, sweeping Frankie into my arms and into step with the other dancers. As always, it's a joy to twist and turn with her following gracefully in my arms. "You're being naughty, Miss Beaumonde."

"I know." She looks pleased with herself. "What are you going to do about it?"

"Find a way to shut that sinful mouth." My body tightens when she licks her lips. I need to find a private corner, stat.

"Well, well, who is this?" A young man in military dress emerges from the crowd. "Aren't you going to introduce me to your lady?"

"Franz." I face the last person I wanted to see.

My brother.

* * *

Frankie

A YOUNGER, less polished version of Benedict stands between us and the rest of the dancers. He's tall and broad-shouldered, smartly dressed in the olive green of the New Arcadian military. But his dark hair is tousled, and he's holding a beer bottle. I didn't even know they served beer at a ball.

"Well, Benny?" He smirks.

"You're blocking our way." Benedict switches me to his other side, putting himself between me and the man. His brother, if my guess is correct.

"Come on, introduce me," he goads, flashing a dimple. He's handsome enough, I guess, in a bland, frat boy way.

I nudge Benedict.

He blows out a breath. "Miss Beaumonde, my brother. The Marquis Dupree."

"See, that wasn't so hard," Franz mocks. Sibling rivalry aside, Franz is a jerkhole. I seriously consider punching him, right in the dimple. Probably wouldn't make the best first impression.

Franz downs the rest of his beer and sets the empty bottle on the tray of a passing waiter. He looks me up and down, and I get the impression he doesn't like what he sees. But he keeps the cocky expression pinned to his face as he comes forward, hand out. "Dance with me?"

"I don't think…" I look to Benedict, but he's shut down, doing his best imitation of a statue.

Franz reaches past him and leads me into the dance. "So you're the fiancée."

"And you're the fuck up," I say, smiling as sweet as can be. Anyone watching will think we're having a friendly chat.

Franz blinks.

That's right, I'm not impressed by you.

"Very nice," he drawls. "Does Benny know you're this feisty? I don't take him as the type to let his woman talk to him like that."

"He lets me do what I want. And don't call him that. His name is Benedict."

Franz cocks his head at me. "You call him Benedict? He lets you?"

"Like I said, he doesn't *let* me do anything. I'm my own person."

"Pretty sure of yourself. I guess you think you can get away with anything, now that you've hooked a duke." And, for the first time, he lets his true coldness show. His sneer looks familiar. I've seen it on Benedict before.

Maybe these royal types do learn it at school.

"Who says I hooked him?" I act breezy, keeping my steps light and in time with the beat. "Maybe he hooked me."

Franz leads me in a complicated set of turns. To his credit, he dances like he was born to waltz. "My brother's never lifted a finger unless it gets him closer to the crown. And now he's engaged? To a commoner? I don't believe it."

"Believe this," I flip him the bird, making sure to include my ring finger sporting the giant sparkling rock along with the middle one. "And now I'm done dancing with you." I shrug him off and stroll away, heading straight for the huge doors leading outside. I need fresh air.

Benedict appears on the balcony a few seconds later. "Frankie? Is everything all right?"

Suddenly the prospect of going back into the crowded ballroom is too much to bear. "I don't want to be here anymore."

"Let's take a walk." He offers his arm, frowning.

We stroll down the wide steps to the garden. Ahead, the moonlight glimmers on the path and the dark expanse of the water.

I sense the tautness in Benedict's body, but I appreciate him waiting until I've had a chance to drink in the moonlight.

He leads me into the shadows by the boathouse. A few men are working inside, setting something up. Benedict finds a dark corner and faces me, taking my hands. "What did Franz say to you?"

I pause before answering. I'm not entirely sure how to sum up the conversation. "He insinuated that I was a gold-digger. Out for your money. Or title. Or whatever."

"He dares…" Benedict swivels, transforming into a tuxedo-wearing warrior, ready to rampage.

I pull him back. "No, please. It's not worth it. Benedict." I touch his cheek and he turns his attention fully to me. "Let's just avoid him in the future."

"We'll be seeing our fair share of him. I'll make it clear he's to treat you with respect."

"No, it's okay. I think he didn't know what to make of me." I tuck a fallen strand of hair behind my ear. "He said I'm not your type."

"Hmm," Benedict grumbles.

"It's true, isn't it?" I realize I'm twisting the ring on my finger, and force my hands down. "I'm not your type."

Benedict looks out at the water for a long while. "I would have thought that before I met you."

"You can tell me the truth—"

"I would have been wrong." He draws me closer, his hand pressing my lower back until he's holding me like we're about to dance. I lean into him, letting his body surround me. Strong shoulders, solid chest, gentle hands. A girl could find a worse source of comfort.

I slide my arms around his waist and let my head droop until my face rubs the silk of his lapels. In the quiet, the only sound is the water lapping at the dock.

"Frankie." His chest swells under my cheek.

I tip my head back to take him in. "Benedict."

He brushes my hair back with a reverent hand. His thumb strokes my forehead, smoothes over my left eyebrow. "No matter how long you take to get ready, you always have this unruly eyebrow. This one refuses to conform." His thumb moves back and forth, teasing the line of my brow. "Do you know what that means?"

I lift my other eyebrow. "You have an eyebrow fetish?

He doesn't seem to hear me. "I want to kiss it all the damn time. Possibly bite it." His hand drops to my lips and his thumb repeats the movement, rubbing over my lower lip.

Back and forth, back and forth. "I want to make it behave. Make *you* behave."

"And how will you do that, Your Grace?" I try for snarky and confident, but his hard body presses against mine, awakening it, and my voice escapes in a breathy rush.

Benedict bends his face close to mine.

Then a creak on the dock makes him snap towards an intruder.

A man in livery bows. "Sir, excuse us. We're about to start the fireworks." He motions to the men working in the boathouse.

With a nod, Benedict draws me away, towards the water. We walk slowly to the end of the dock. Faint strains from the orchestra follow us, but the rest of the world seems distant. There's nothing but me in my big ball gown, him in his tux, and a thousand stars sparkling like diamonds in the night.

Out on the water, the breeze is cooler. I shiver, rubbing my gloved arms. Benedict jerks off his tux jacket and tucks me into it. The sleeves droop past my hands, just as they did the last time I wore his jacket. I push them back, chuckling.

"Does something amuse you?"

"The day we met. You were so angry with me."

"I had no idea what was happening."

"I came in like a wrecking ball." I wrap my arms around myself and because I'm wearing Benedict's jacket, surrounded by his scent, it feels like he's hugging me.

"And my life was never the same."

Movement on the gravel path beyond the boathouse catches my eye. A young man in military dress is striding towards the water. Franz.

I beam up at Benedict and angle myself so Benedict's back is to his brother. I can only hope Franz didn't come down here to yell at us.

Fortunately, Benedict is distracted. By me. He brings my

hand to his lips. He doesn't kiss it, just rubs them back and forth against my skin. "You're not a wrecking ball. You're a blast of fresh air in a stuffy room."

I snort and arch a brow.

"All right," he amends. "More like a hurricane, ripping me from my foundations."

"Lovely. Fantastic compliment, comparing me to a storm. Full scale destruction, that's me."

"And yet…" His deep voice is soft, wondering. "And yet I wouldn't have it any other way."

The wind picks up, blowing my hair across my face. And Benedict is there, cupping my cheeks with his elegant hands, smoothing my wild tresses. When the wind dies, he doesn't remove his hands.

"Frankie." He dips his head and claims my mouth.

The kiss detonates.

I barely hear the explosion in the sky. Fireworks burst above us, popping to life and dying in a blaze of colored sparks. We kiss again and I cling to him, my hands sliding up the muscled plane of his back and grabbing handfuls of his fancy shirt. I want to climb him, and he seems game.

Until he tears away, and jerks me off the dock. I fall backwards, watching the incoming firework shriek like a missile as it heads straight for us.

CHAPTER 8

THE RIVER in high summer isn't cold, but it's still a shock. I keep hold of Frankie. There was no time to explain why I launched us off the dock. The least I can do is keep her from drowning.

There's a low boom as a firework explodes close to the water. I grab Frankie, pushing us under to protect us from the bright sparks.

We come up gasping.

I kick madly, treading water, fighting to keep our heads up. We're not far from shore, but a wool tux and dress shoes aren't ideal swimwear. And in her ballgown, Frankie is worse off than I am. I haul her along, swimming until I can touch the bottom.

Then I drag us out of the water. The fireworks are still bursting merrily overhead. If anyone saw us nearly get decapitated by an aerial, they don't come running to see if we survived.

"Oh my god," Frankie gasps. My tux jacket is long gone, but she's still in sodden gloves and two hundred pounds of wet tulle. She lolls on the grass, coughing. I pound her back until she weakly waves me away. "It's okay, I'm okay. What just happened?"

"A firework. It came right at us."

"I saw that. Were they aiming for us?"

"An accident. A trick of the wind. Are you all right?"

"Fine. Help me." She tears at her gloves. I roll them off and discard them. They're ruined anyway. Then I make short work of her skirts, tearing the dress clean off.

Underneath she's wearing a merry widow and a bloomer petticoat thing made of fabric so thin and fine, it's now translucent.

My adrenaline's pumping, and in an instant, all that vigor rushes straight to my groin. I stagger, staring at my fiancée. She's a goddess in the moonlight, her wet skin luminous and her hair black as the velvet sky. My brunette Venus, emerging from the river instead of the Cyprian sea. Soaking wet instead of surfing sea foam.

It hurts, how much I want her.

"My god." I gather her into my arms. She seems smaller when she's soaking wet, without fashionable armor. I kiss her forehead and wrap my arms around her. She clings to me. The only thing that keeps me from ravishing her on the lawn is the knowledge that eventually, someone is bound to see. And if the wind picks up again, she might catch a chill.

This is a disaster. We can't go back into the ball. My only hope is to get her across the lawn with no one noticing, and signal someone to find our car.

"Come on." I help her up the bank and lift her past the gravel path. She's barefoot, her body shivering violently.

But then I realize she's not shivering—she's laughing. Of course she is. Only Frankie would find this funny.

"Karma," she says, pointing to her ruined undergarments. "For all the Miss Carrot contestants."

"Your Grace." A man in livery rushes up. "Are you all right?" He gapes at us, Frankie in particular.

"What the hell was that?" I tighten my hold on Frankie to keep from tearing him apart. His mouth hangs open as he drinks in her dishabille.

"We had a little problem with—"

"Never mind. Give me your jacket." I snap my fingers when the man is too slow. I drape Frankie in the red livery, and block her bodily from his view. "Go inside and find a man named Daniel Fitzroy. Tell him to call the car and meet us out front. Now."

"I guess I'd call my first ball a success," Frankie says as we trudge up the hill, sneaking around the building and giving a wide berth to the light thrown from the great windows. "Not great, but I survived."

"Forgive me."

"Ah, no." She brushes off my apology. "If anything, it was my fault. I wanted to go outside."

We're almost at the front of the building. Ahead is the long line of cars waiting for their owners. And I curse myself because I should have been more specific. Our limo is waiting—directly in front of the steps. Steps that are thronged in a thicket of reporters.

"Damn. Damn, damn, damn." I grip Frankie's hand. "We'll have to make a run for it."

"Ready when you are."

It's no use. As soon as we get close, the light falls on us. A reporter starts out of his skin. He nudges his buddy, who almost drops his camera. Almost. Another two seconds, and their cameras swing up and start clicking.

"Out of our way," I order. "Now."

They back away, only to be joined by fifteen more. I throw up a hand and shield Frankie as best I can, gritting my teeth to keep from cursing the lot of them.

"Your Grace!" Daniel shouts, pushing to the front of the fray. He sees us, and horror streaks across his face. "This way." He rips off his own tux jacket, holding it over our heads as we run for the car.

"Your Grace, what happened?" shout the reporters. "A moment for questions? Did you decide to go swimming? Was it your fiancée's idea? Is this an American tradition?"

Frankie dives into the car with me on her bare heels.

"Go," Daniel gasps to the driver. "I'll run interference." He slams the door, and the driver speeds us off into the night.

"Well," Frankie says, collapsing back onto the car seat. "That was fucked."

"My foul-mouthed Beatrice." I scoot closer so I can run my hands over her arms, checking to see if she's really okay. When I'm satisfied, I cup her cheek. "You're sure you're all right?"

"I'm sure. Wet and full of adrenaline. There are worse things to be." Her eyes sparkle, and I can't hold back anymore. I draw her face to mine and kiss her. Her chilled skin warms to my touch. She sips at my lips, her tongue tasting me. I'm so stiff, I'm dizzy.

I draw back for a breath. "Where were we?"

"You were about to make love to my eyebrows. We kept getting interrupted."

"Ah, yes." I stroke said eyebrow, and kiss it for good measure. When I sit back, Frankie looks tired, pleased, but a little guarded.

"Come to bed with me," I whisper.

"That's a bad idea." Her gaze sidles from mine and she scoots back on the seat, away from me.

"Why?" I battle my arousal, gripping the seat to keep from reaching for her.

Her good mood slips away entirely. "Don't you remember? This is all fake."

* * *

Frankie

As soon as the car slows in front of the house, I hop out. It takes me a moment to realize it's not my house. Daniel didn't think we needed to move in together, but he did recommend we overnight in the same house once in a while. He even had me pack a small bag of my things to stow at Benedict's for this express purpose. But planning is one thing. Actually doing it might be dangerous.

Before I can back away, the duke is behind me. He reaches past me to unlock the door.

"After you, Lady Beatrice." He steps back and sweeps his arm to indicate I should go first. I stare at the dark square of the doorway like it's the gates of hell.

I shouldn't. I really shouldn't.

"You're cold and wet, and we've been through an ordeal," Benedict says softly. "Let me take care of you. Nothing will happen if you don't want it to."

"I know that," I scoff, and enter the house. Benedict is a gentleman. I'm more afraid of myself. What I want and what is wise are so far apart, they live in different countries.

But I can't resist another cuddle session on the couch, with Benedict fussing over me.

That is exactly where I end up: dry, and dressed in a pair of Duke University sweats, on the loveseat in his private study. Benedict covers me in a blanket, smoothing it over me. Just like last time.

Then he hands me a glass of brandy. Just like the last time. There are crinkles in the corner of his eyes. "You don't have to drink it."

"Seriously?" I regard the amber liquid. I'd say a prayer to St. Francis, but the saint washed his hands of me a week ago.

Benedict settles himself next to me, far enough away I can take in his casual posture. Portrait of a lord in repose. Out of a suit, he looks younger but just as powerful. He sips his brandy, looking thoughtful.

A long silence passes, and then he recites, *"Nature never framed a woman's heart of prouder stuff than that of Beatrice. Disdain and scorn ride sparkling in her eyes, misprizing what they look on, and her wit values itself so highly that to her all matter else seems weak."*

"Someone's been studying their Shakespeare." I smile into my glass. "If this is your idea of foreplay, it's working."

He looks at me then, and I feel the full weight of his hunger. "Come to bed with me, Frankie."

My stomach turns to stone. I lower my brandy, cradling it to my chest like a shield over my heart. "I should check on Elvis."

"He's fine. I hired not one but two parrot sitters. They have veterinary degrees. Ornithological specialities."

Tempting. It is so tempting. He'll kiss me, do marvelous things to my body, and exit stage right, leaving my heart on the floor.

"Benedict, this is fake. All of it."

"It doesn't have to be." His dark eyes bore into mine. He seems sincere.

I set down my glass. That's my cue. *"I had rather hear my dog bark at a crow than a man swear he loves me,"* I quote Lady

Beatrice. I planned these lines, anticipated them. I expected them to feel triumphant, but they leave me hollow.

I rise, and he rises with me. I head to the door, but my steps slow as I reach it, as if I'm waiting for something.

Benedict obliges, right on cue. "Who said anything about love?"

He's standing by the fireplace, staring into his glass as if the dark liquid will show the future. Portrait of a devil, ready to make a deal.

I shouldn't. I really shouldn't.

But I do. I turn slowly, and walk to him. I'm barefoot and so is he, but I'm so much shorter. "All right, Your Grace. What do you propose?"

enedict

HER DARK BROWN eyes tilt up at me, taunting me. Her damp hair falls in a riot down her shoulders. Her lips are full and her head's tipped back, showing the smooth, pale line of her throat. I shouldn't, I really shouldn't. But I'm going to. I'm a duke; I should be used to getting what I want. But my royal life has never been about indulgence. Not when it's all hanging by a thread.

It occurs to me I could cut that thread. Let go, and dedicate my life to pursuing what I really want. Starting with Frankie.

Frankie sways closer, then halts. She can sense hesitation, and I've remained still too long. I step forward and plunge my hand into the dark fall of her hair. "I propose this," I say, and lower my lips to hers. I mean it to be a coaxing kiss, but as per usual, Frankie's scent and presence, the pure sparkling essence of her, burns through all my control. I tighten my fingers in her hair, guiding her closer. Her lips part beneath mine, and I plunder. Her mouth is soft and silk and sinful. I lick up the taste. She whimpers, and I realize my fist in her hair has her pulled up to tiptoe.

"This is how it will be, pet," I murmur. "I'm not going to hold back." I'm not sure I can. I typically can control myself, do what's expected in the bedroom, no more, no less, but this is Frankie. She wreaks havoc in every area of my life. Why stop now?

"So that's what you're into," she mutters. "I should've guessed. You like to take charge." She melts against me, pushing higher to nuzzle me, just begging to be taken in hand. "I love it."

"Naughty girl."

"Mmmm, yes." Now she's trying to climb me. "Keep talking, like that."

I tug her head back by her hair again, gentle but firm. "You're not in charge right now." I take a chance and slip my right hand between her legs, into the pair of sweatpants that hang ridiculously big on her. She's bare underneath, no panties. Bare and deliciously wet.

"Oh," she gasps and teeters up higher on her tiptoes. I fondle her soft, juicy folds and find the entrance to her sex. I dip a long finger inside, twisting to collect her essence. Then I remove my hand and let her watch, wide-eyed, as I lick her off my finger.

"Oh, yes." I hold her gaze as I purr. "I'm going to want more of that."

She whimpers again, wobbling on weak legs. I scoop her up and carry her to the nearest chair. She's not ready for bed, not yet. An overstuffed Chesterfield is just the thing.

Eventually I'll claim her on every surface in my home. My cock twitches at the thought.

She helps me remove the sweatpants, wriggling backwards onto the deep leather seat, her brown eyes deliciously wide. I have unfettered access to her lower half, and she knows it.

My hand shackles her ankle and she jumps. "Easy," I soothe, stroking her ankle. I wait for her skittishness to subside before drawing her closer. "Come to me, yes, that's it," I say, though I'm not giving her any choice. Her legs tense and scrabble a little bit, then relax as I pull her down the seat so she's lying flat on her back, hair tousled and spilling over the leather, her long legs coltish and awkward as she realizes she's laid out like a buffet before me. She tries to press her knees together at the last moment and I tsk. "Now, now. Open to me." I take hold of her knees and ease them apart. Yes. That's the sight I want, her pink folds flushed, her center glossy with juices as her body readies itself for me.

I spread her legs wide and kneel between them before they can close. One hand props up her inner thigh, and the other pets her pussy. She squirms.

"Be good," I order, as if that'll work. She rolls her eyes.

I smack her center, lightly. Her head flies back and her body seizes up. "Oh my god!"

"*Your Grace* will do."

She rolls her eyes. "All this power's gone to your head."

"Do you mind?" I pet her pussy again, the lightest swipe of my thumb over her folds. And she relaxes right into my touch.

"Mmm, no. I don't mind." And then she adds, more softly, "It makes me feel safe."

I kiss her knee. "Good. No more talking now, unless you want me to stop." I kiss a trail up to her sex, and spread her open with my thumbs. Her pussy is pink and perfect, her clitoris standing at attention. I lower my head to lick up a taste. She's got her hands over her mouth, but adorable little squeaks sneak past her fingers. I pause to tell her, "You can make all the noise you like." Then I flick my tongue against her clit.

"Oh." Her abs tighten under my hand as she erupts onto my tongue. I dip my head and plunge my tongue into her pussy, filling my senses with her sweet musk. Her channel contracts, seeking stimulation. I sit back and wipe her wetness from my beard with one hand. My other keeps stroking the sensitive spot right alongside her clit, keeping her convulsing. After a minute, I press my palm gently against her sex, grounding her.

"That was so good," she sighs. Her cheeks are lovely, flushed pink with pleasure. Pink like her sweet pussy.

I lick her taste off my lips. "That was just the beginning."

I rise and scoop her up, carrying her swiftly to my bedroom. The moment I cross the threshold into the dark room, I feel the change. Like a distant bell tolling, filling me with a sense of rightness. Frankie belongs here, in my most intimate space. My inner sanctum. Maybe one day, I can let all my walls down and tell her my secrets. Something tells me she'd be the one, the only one, who'd understand.

But now's not the time for all that. Her dark head is a comfortable weight on my shoulder. She makes not a murmur as I carry her through my room. Perhaps I should stop things and check on her, make sure she's thinking clearly enough to consent.

But when I set her down on the bed, she reaches for me.

"Frankie?"

"Benedict," she sighs and tugs me closer. "Make love to me."

* * *

Frankie

I stretch out on the bed, tugging on Benedict's shirt to

bring him with me. He obeys willingly, stretching out over me. I spread my legs wide and he settles between them, a delicious weight.

I've just come faster with him than I have with any man. My pussy is still fluttering with the aftermath.

But I'm greedy. I want it all.

"It's been a while since I've done this," I admit.

"Oh, Frankie, I'm going to make it so good."

I close my eyes and let him settle over me, his presence like a warm blanket. I don't need to think any more. Benedict's got me and I can soar, trusting that, when the time comes, he'll take me gently back to Earth.

"Just follow my lead." And he dips his head and kisses me.

I sigh into him. We've always been good together. The attraction was there right from the beginning, and fighting it only made it stronger. He's sipping at my lips, slanting his head to drink down more of me. I wrap my legs around his hips and rock upwards. My sensitive naughty girl bits brush against his hard boy bits through his pants. He sucks in a breath.

"Wicked girl," he says. "I'm going to take care of you."

"I know," I say. "You're not like the other guys."

His hands pause, and I realize I've said too much. To distract him, I slip my hands under his soft t-shirt and find bare skin. My eyes pop wide. There's quite a lot of muscle under here.

"What's this?" I tug up his shirt and stare at the beautiful expanse of eight pack abs. "You've been hiding all this… under your suits? It should be a crime." His muscles flex under my palms and then he catches my wrists, pulling my hands away so he can remove my shirt. I'm so distracted by my short glimpse of his amazing muscles that I let him. Then I realize I'm now naked. Unlike Mr. Hidden Muscles, I do not have a sleek and sexy body, ready to model on a magazine cover of Beautiful People R' Us.

I go to cover my chest and he catches my wrists again. "No," he says. "Show me." Something about his commands makes me want to obey. I drop my hands.

He reaches over and flicks on the bedside lamp. I flinch but the light is gentle and warm. We're still deep in our silent, cozy cocoon.

"So beautiful." He traces along the swell of my breast, and I shiver. "You're sensitive?"

"Very," I say, but I don't have to answer. He dips his head and now I'm writhing under him.

He gathers my wrists in a loose grip and pins them above my head.

"Leave them there." He gives me a stern look. I giggle. He's being his arrogant self, but instead of annoying me, it makes me wet. He purses his lips. "So naughty."

I wriggle happily. "I like being naughty with you."

"Perhaps I should do something about that," he murmurs cryptically, and kisses me again. He lets loose my wrists and without thinking, I start to draw my arms down.

"Uh-uh." He pins them again on either side of my head and fixes me with a stern look. "Now stay. Next time there'll be consequences."

Hello, Mr. Control. "Next time there'll be consequences," I parrot back to him in a snooty accent, then gasp as his palm catches the underside of my bottom. I arc up off the bed. "Benedict!"

"Yes, my lady?" He squeezes my ass, palming it and massaging away the sting. The shock recedes, leaving a reciprocal ache in my pussy. "I warned you," he says in the most deliciously arrogant tone.

"I guess you did." I purr, arching into his touch. I feel sultry and sexy, a wanton goddess. No wham bam, thank you man here. Benedict has already eaten me out, and now he's being stern. Makes me want to think of new ways to be cheeky. What a fantastically fun game.

"Be good," he mutters darkly, and lowers his head to nuzzle at my breasts. I grip the bed sheets to keep from grabbing his dark head, and give myself over to the sensations. He licks and nibbles around my nipples, browsing over my bosoms until they're swollen and aching in the best way.

"I've wanted to do this for so long," he says when I'm panting. He palms my pussy, stimulating me with sure strokes at the same time as he licks around my nipple. He has me writhing in seconds. His touch is so certain, so sure. He already knows his way around my body.

He breaks away before I orgasm, and though I want to groan, I giggle instead.

Benedict arches a brow. "What's so funny?"

"We're—what's the phrase again? *Anticipating* our wedding vows," I say. "Wedding vows that will never happen." And I crack up. For some reason, it's funny to me.

His face softens as he watches me laugh then he says with mock sternness, "If you're thinking about that, I'm not doing a good enough job." And he dips his head and kisses me again.

His tongue strokes the inside of my mouth, teasing mine. My pussy throbs with anticipation of him penetrating me in a different way.

Then he pulls away and murmurs, "So delicious, so delightful, so naughty."

I want to grab his face and order him to fuck me but I have a feeling that will get me in trouble. *Consequences,* as he says. So instead I raise my hips again, rocking upwards, silently begging for his cock.

He reaches down and frees himself. His member is warm and hard against my thigh. My pussy clenches again. I'm dripping, ready for him. A flash of warning goes through my mind. *Maybe we shouldn't take this step.*

It's just sex, I argue against that prim and prudish voice. *I deserve to have a little fun.* I've been on my own for so long.

Remember what happened last time? The warning voice persists, but I push it away.

You can't trust these rich boys. But Benedict isn't a boy. He's a man.

"I'm on birth control." I tell him.

"Good." His voice is ragged, his control slipping. "Condoms for now." The drawer to the bedside table is open and he already has a condom in hand. He must have grabbed it when I was having an argument with the prudent, cautious, and totally boring part of myself.

He pauses to roll the condom on and every thought flies out of my head when I get a good glimpse of his dick. It's hard and large and proud, with an arrogant tilt to it. Can a penis be arrogant? Benedict's manages it. Of course it does.

I giggle again. *Arrogant prick. Literally.* I don't dare say anything out loud, but he catches my grin and shakes his head.

"You are incorrigible."

I'm about to repeat my firm stance that I am entirely corrigible and *will you please fuck me now?* when he slides inside. It burns a little and he goes slowly, waiting for me to stretch around him. It has been a while, and I'm glad I warned him.

He rocks a little, stretching me out. The inner walls of my pussy kiss along his cock, welcoming him into my tight heat. I want to feel him deep inside me, and he's big enough that when he's all the way in, I will. I rest my cheek against his pec and cling to him. I've totally forgotten to keep my hands locked down. He's going to have to tie me up to get me to obey. Maybe that's something we'll save for next time.

"Feeling all right?" He checks in on me. Such a gentleman. Will he ask 'please' before he comes? I hope not.

He's seated deep inside me. His body is heavy over mine, but he's holding most of his weight on taut forearms. I slide my hand up around his neck, stroking his thick hair as my tight channel adjusts to his girth. Then I grip his shoulders and crane my neck to lick his ear.

"Fuck me, Benedict. Fuck me hard." I want to feel him the next day.

A sharp inhale. Then he glides almost all the way out. A pause, and then he slams back in. I topple over into orgasm with a shout.

He removes my hands from hanging on to him and pins them to either side of my head. His cheeks are flushed. His dark eyes glitter. He's beautiful and wicked, a fallen angel. His dick is doing sinful things to my insides. Another orgasm rises again as he grinds down, somehow hitting my clit and my G-spot all at once. He drags his cock out slowly. Sparks fly and then fireworks explode in my body.

His grip is hard on my wrists as he drives into me. Each thrust slams me further up the bed. White lights dance behind my eyes—the aftermath of the last orgasm, or the beginning of another.

Then he presses his forehead to mine and groans. His cock feels bigger inside me, throbbing, pumping his cum into the condom. His lips catch mine and then he lets my arms free. Immediately I wrap my arms around his broad shoulders.

"Control freak much?" I whisper and he laughs back at me, letting me tug him down to rest his weight on me. He's heavier than I'd expect—must be all those muscles he's hidden all this time under his suit.

He turns his head and kisses between my breasts, then rises to deal with the condom. The second he rises, I miss his weight on me. I'm not sure how I got here, into the duke's bed, my skin tingling from the orgasms he gave me, but now I'm here, I don't want to leave. Our false engagement, the vows I made to not let him get close, even the crazy night at the ball with the fireworks—it all seems so far away.

And then Benedict is back and helping me up to give me a drink of water. He strokes my hair back and kisses me again. And that leads to us tangled together, skin on sweaty skin. Safe and warm and happy. He rolls and traps me with a heavy leg over mine. "Stay with me," he whispers. In answer, I snuggle deeper into his chest. He reaches over to click off the light, then puts his arm around me. Within seconds, I'm asleep.

* * *

Frankie

IT'S awkward sleeping with someone through the night. Maybe they move too much, or you move too. Someone's gonna hog the covers or sprawl over more their fair share of the bed. The heat, the sweat, the way two unfamiliar bodies knock together—there are so many micro-discomforts that prod you awake, and leave you wishing for your own bed. My ex, Ben, was a sweet guy, but he and I only spent the night together in the same bed a few times. Enough for me to realize it wasn't comfortable. The guy I was with before Ben was the first guy I'd ever been with. My first, back when I was young and believed in fairytales. He and I were always in a rush, sneaking around. There was no time for cuddles or intimacy. Looking back, that was the biggest red flag. When a guy tries to hustle you out of sight so parents or staff don't know he's meeting with you, you know it's not going to end well.

But I don't want to dwell on that.

Morning light filters through the blinds and I wake slowly, cradled in the muted blue shadows of Benedict's cozy bedroom. His big body slumbers next to me, a mountain of warmth and comfort. I stretch slowly, unwilling to leave. At first he kept me tucked against him all night, as if preventing me from sneaking off. At some point he moved to the side but still kept a big hand splayed over my stomach possessively. I slept deeply. I haven't slept that way since I was a girl —without worry or troubled dreams. Without a care.

Shifting carefully to my side, I face my slumbering fiancé. His dark hair falls over his face and firm lips. His long lashes fan under his eyes. He left his shirt off, and I get a chance to properly examine his muscled chest. The smooth contours are sprinkled with dark, coarse hair. I remember with delight how his chest hair rubbed against my skin, chafing it. And my wrists still hold the memory of Benedict's fingers shackling them, pinning them to the bed.

He's beautiful in slumber. Maybe it's his size but he's still a solid, forceful presence, even asleep. Maybe that's why I slept so well—my subconscious relaxed, knowing my bedmate could protect me.

How in the hell has this man remained unmarried and eligible for so long?

I want to touch his face, stroke his features, but I don't want to wake him. His body is heavy with muscle—but when does he have time to work out? He rules his body with the same discipline as everything else.

I don't totally understand the succession rules of this kingdom and the huge headache of their complicated big deal and pomp and ceremony. But Benedict would make a great king. The country would be safe in his hands.

I misjudged him as arrogant. I hope others don't make the same mistake. Yes, Benedict's had every privilege, but he's worked so hard to prove himself. He deserves to rule. I hope I can help him achieve that, or at least make things easier for him.

But first a bath, or at least a shower. I'm a little sore in the best way. Besides, the duke might wake up presentable, but I need a little more help.

When I walk into the gorgeous master bath, I catch sight of myself in the mirror. With my wild mermaid hair, I look like a figure in a John William Waterhouse painting. My cheeks are flushed as if I've just orgasmed. Desire certainly is a great beautifier.

Not that the duke ever had a problem being attracted to me. It was always there, despite our wishes. I smirk at my reflection before heading to the gorgeous, Roman style tiled tub. Next to it is a wonder of chrome and glass and technology—a steam shower with about seven hundred knobs and buttons to regulate water pressure. Bath or shower, which to choose?

I decide on the bath, because if I press the wrong knob in the ultra-modern shower, it might shoot me into outer space. Again, the tub is right near the window, but the natural light and view of the tree outside is welcome.

Until I realize there's a man in jeans and a t-shirt sitting on a branch, a few feet away.

We see each other at the same time. I shriek and grab the sheet I wrapped myself in. It shrouds me like I'm a Roman statue swathed in wet drapery—revealing more than it conceals.

He startles and fumbles for the camera dangling from a strap around his neck.

"What the actual fuck?" I shriek. My voice reverberates in

the marble splendor of the bathroom. *"Fuck-fuck-fuck-fuck-fuck..."* It's not ladylike to swear, but what the actual fuck?

I step to the window, about to throw up the sash and give him a piece of my mind, when Benedict's half-awake bellow rings out. "Frankie?"

The paparazzo jerks in surprise again, and this time it overbalances him. With a cry, he falls from the branch, crashing through foliage.

"What is it? What happened?"

Benedict stumbles into the bathroom as I point to the window and scream, "Call an ambulance!"

CHAPTER 10

rankie

AN HOUR LATER, my ears are still ringing. From the ambulance siren—which sounds different here than in America. From the shouts of the poor photographer—who landed on some shrubbery. "Not badly hurt," Daniel informed us after he spoke to the chief of police. "More than he deserved."

The camera didn't survive intact. Thank goodness.

We're in the car, Benedict and I. Benedict's transformed back into The Duke. I can tell. He was so different—still dominant, but warm and gentle last night. Right now, his profile might as well be carved in stone.

"This cannot stand," he says suddenly.

"It's not your fault." Biting my lip, I take a chance. I wind myself around him, drawing him away from the window into the heat of my body. He allows me to cuddle close, tucking my head under his jaw. His body is big and solid, mine is soft and, I like to think, comforting. We fit together.

After a minute, his shoulders relax a fraction. "They're a problem. It's high time I do something about it."

"The reporters?"

"Yes." His chin moves against my hair. "The paparazzi. The royalty and paparazzi are symbiotic. It's especially apparent in England, where the royals have little more than soft power."

I don't know what to say so I keep resting my head on his chest. The adrenaline from this morning has faded. I'm not tired, but I am a little wrung out.

I'm not quite dozing when Benedict says very, very softly, "My mother loved the spotlight. She gloried in it."

His body is tense again under mine. My eyes widen but I don't move in case I scare him off from saying more.

"It killed her," he adds finally.

I raise my head. This is a serious conversation. "I thought she died in a yachting accident," I say. His fingers clench and unclench until I gather them into mine.

"She did. She was partying. Making a spectacle. Bigger and better, even at the cost of her health. Relationships. And then at the cost of her life."

"I'm sorry," I say softly. My heart aches for the little boy who lost his mother.

No wonder Benedict shuns the limelight or scandal.

"She fought with her husband about it, that very night. I hung at the top of the staircase and listened. It seemed they were always fighting." Benedict's voice is hushed and his eyes are fixed ahead on nothing. On images from the past. He's locked deep in his memories.

I can't stand it. I want to help.

The car rolls on, heading into the country. After we got the reporter into the ambulance and Daniel arrived with more security, Benedict called his great aunt. She insisted we come stay at her estate where we can lie low.

We're cozy and it's private. The divider's up between us and the driver. It usually is.

"How far are we from Lady Ursaline's house?" I ask.

"Twenty minutes. Why?"

I lay a hand on his thigh, marveling at the muscle under the suit slacks. He's more lean than bulky, but now I've seen how cut he is, I can't forget. I slide my hand up until my fingers brush the bulge in his slacks. He's hard, as I expected. I haven't been strategically pressing my boobs against him under the pretense of 'comfort' for nothing.

"Frankie." If he's trying for stern, he's failing. It comes out breathy. A little desperate. "Darling."

"Darling? That's new. I like it." And I slip off the seat to my knees. I position myself between his legs, looking up at him from under my lashes. He doesn't say anything, but his chest rises and falls with labored breath.

I go to unbutton his slacks and take him out, and he catches my chin. "No." His thumb brushes my lower lip. My tongue darts out automatically and licks at his skin. His eyes hood.

"If we do this, we do this my way." His voice rasps.

"All right." As brash as I'm behaving, it's nice to just take orders. Not think for a little while.

Benedict gives a crisp nod and hits the button that allows him to speak to the driver. "McKinney? Take the long way," he orders, and waits for McKinney's assent before muting the com channel and gathering up my hair, tugging me back. "I'm in charge," he tells me.

I nod, a little curious.

"Unbutton your blouse."

Now I'm breathing hard. But there's no time to be nervous. All I have to do is listen and obey.

I slip the pearl buttons free. I'm wearing a lacy bralette underneath. Part of my new wardrobe. I never thought there would be a button-down shirt or bralette that would fit my boobs and actually look good. The benefits of a stylist and tailor.

Benedict regards the lace with a calm arrogance that I would call dismissive, if I wasn't almost eye level with his giant erection. The aloofness is part of his social armor, I realize. His need to be in control. Perhaps the loss of his mother at a young age.

But I can psychoanalyze him later.

"Do you want me to take it off? "I gesture to the bralette.

"No…" He reaches out a long finger and traces the lace. "Lovely. I think, just…" He tugs the bralette down, tucking it under my breasts. The white lace pushes my breasts up and out and turns my cleavage into a cavernous wonder. Benedict strokes the tops of my breasts like they've been put on a platter and offered up for his enjoyment. I feel like a toy, in the best way. It makes me so wet.

"Yes, I think that'll do." Benedict finishes arranging me to his liking. I'm breathing heavily from the casual fondling. He leans back in the seat, lounging like a bored king. "Now. Take out my cock."

* * *

BENEDICT

FRANKIE LICKS HER LIPS, frowning with concentration. I force myself to relax into a casual pose, controlling every breath as she slowly undoes my pants and draws my boxer briefs down. It's all I can do to stop myself lunging for her, laying her out on the floor of the limo, and rutting her.

She takes hold of my member and it jerks in her hand.

Anticipation. Control, I remind myself sternly. Frankie's

hands are so small and uncertain, holding my dick.

When she frees it completely, she widens her eyes at me as if to say, *I'm going to have to fit all of that in my mouth?*

I nod. "Lick the tip."

But this is Frankie, and she's up to any challenge. With a sly brow arched, she runs her tongue around the head, then closes her mouth over me. She hums as she sucks hard.

I tug her hair. "Not so fast." Her naughty mouth on my cock is an unholy temptation, but I want this to last. I inhale harshly, gathering my control. "Lick up the side." I guide her head down and she obeys, her coy tongue snaking out to curl around my length. Her lashes flutter when she gets a taste. I force my fingers to relax in her hair. "Yes, good." I can't hide the fact that I'm breathing heavily, my muscles turned to iron. "Now the other side."

And now, I pull her head forward. I don't have to say anything else. Her mouth glides all the way down, and I lose every thought in my mind.

* * *

Frankie

BENEDICT'S COCK is warm between my lips. His fingers in my hair flex as I gobble him down. He wasn't expecting this. I'd grin if my mouth wasn't full of him.

He's big—so big, I can't get the fingers of one hand around him. I try not to think of the intimidating girth and just focus on swirling my tongue around, sucking as hard as I can. His moans above me increase, and I know he's gone. I cradle his balls in my hand, stroking them. My nails scratch lightly and he hisses in a breath. He takes over, forcing my head down a little bit further. I let my shoulders and neck go loose, and let him take control. It's nice not to have to think, to worry whether I'm pleasing him. When I choke a little bit, he lets me back off. My eyes are watering and I'm glad I didn't put on mascara before we raced out of the house. It'd be streaming down my cheeks like the aftermath of a telenovela actress's dramatic tears.

"Frankie," Benedict growls. "I'm going to..." His abs tighten and his hips draw up, pumping his cock deep as he grunts softly. I let my jaw relax as he fills my mouth. I swallow and keep my lips around him, enjoying his shudders. When the aftershocks fade, I come off his cock with a pop and lick my lips. His features are relaxed, completely free of the strain that twisted them before.

I stay on my knees, catching my breath. I want to duck my head to his knee and curl up at his feet like a cat. Enjoy the safe and quiet, this submissive moment.

Benedict strokes my lips, the corner of my mouth. "Was that too much?"

I shake my head. "I liked it."

He opens his arms and I crawl up to snuggle against him. His taste is rich, a bit salty, in my mouth. He kisses the top of my head

"Do you like that?" I ask. "Taking control?"

"Yes," he says. "You'll tell me if you don't like it?"

I shrug. "I actually prefer it. I can stand on my own two feet, but in the bedroom... it's nice to give myself over to someone. Someone I trust."

"I'm honored you trust me." His arms squeeze tight and relax. Outside the car windows, the grand shape of Lady Ursaline's manor has come into view.

"You're not like the others," I add without thinking. "You're unlike anyone I've ever met."

He frowns as if he wants to ask me more, but the car stops and it's time for us to get out.

Lady Ursaline isn't present, but her staff greets us. We have a whole wing of the house to ourselves, and lunch is already laid out. Benedict declines the tour in favor of catching up on his emails, but sends me off with a kiss. To my delight there's a large theater room near our set of rooms.

I return to the cozy parlor where I left Benedict working. The light streaming through the windows is hazy and welcoming. It's a perfect, lazy Sunday afternoon. "I love how these ancient old houses all now have theater rooms."

Benedict nods absently, not looking up from his screen. "Yes, my aunt's close friend had a theater room put in, so she had to have one put in as well." I put a hand on his shoulder and he covers it with his large one. "Do you want to watch a movie?"

"May I?"

"Of course." To my delight, he closes the laptop. "I'll join you."

He lets me select the movie. I waggle my brows at him as the opening credits start playing. "I've always wanted to kiss a man during fireworks."

"I'm sure that can be arranged." He cups the back of my neck, drawing me in for a kiss. It's too early in the movie for the fireworks, but they pop in my belly.

He breaks the kiss all too soon. "Shall I order drinks and popcorn?"

I blink at the movie screen. The kiss made me forget what we were doing. "We can do that?"

He laughs. "Just like a real movie theater. Or so I'm told."

"Wait, have you ever been to one?"

He shakes his head. "Security risk. But we can recreate the experience."

He settles me in a chair and tucks a blanket around me.

"Be good." He boops my nose. I stick out my tongue at him. "Careful," he warns. "Consequences." *Shiver.*

I spend the next few minutes fussing with the cushy double theater seat, figuring out which lever to press to make the divider sink down. We can just hold our drinks and popcorn, or set them aside and do… other things.

Now I just need Benedict back.

There's a creak in the hall, and I pop up. "Need help?" The door's shut, and he might have his hands full.

I open the door, and there is Franz. With his metrosexual haircut and casual clothes, he looks like a member of a boy band. Young, handsome enough, but still a boy. Benedict is a man.

"Franz." I cross my arms. "What a pleasure to see you." My flat tone indicates it's not.

"Oh, it's you. Wots-her-name." He waggles a finger at me. "Froggy. No…" He taps his chin and pretends to think. "Fritzy. No, what is it again? Something masculine."

I roll my eyes. "What do you want, Franz?"

"Just being a good host. Seeing how you're passing the time." He cranes his head to see the movie screen, and scoffs. "My brother can do better than this."

"Better than Hitchcock?" I play dumb. "I picked the movie. Don't blame his taste, blame mine."

His joking behavior falls away and he shoves his hands into his pockets. "You're really going to go through with it?"

"Through with what?" There's an intensity in his eyes I don't like.

"This whole sham. Facade. Fake engagement."

An icy sensation trickles up my spine. "Who says it's fake?"

He shrugs. "People talk. Maybe you're not as good an actress as you think you are. But I'll tell you this, honey," he steps closer, "if you wanted a chance at the throne, you're focusing on the wrong brother."

That makes no sense to me and I'm not sure what to say,

so I stay quiet.

"Haven't you heard?" Franz stretches like a smug cat. "Dear brother Benny is as much of a fake as you are."

"What do you mean?" I ask before I can stop myself.

His eyes light up with glee—he knows he's gotten under my skin. He strolls into the theater room, hands still in his pockets. He's not quite as tall as Benedict but still tall enough to loom over me.

"Here's the deal," he says. "If you want to reel in a real royal, you should consider me."

"What are you talking about?" I repeat. I want to tell Franz he's smoking crack but now he's got me confused. "You're the younger brother. Benedict's next in line for the throne."

Franz taps the side of his nose then points at me, looking sly. "But is he?"

"Yes." Suspense makes me grouchy. I prop my hands on my hips. "From all my understanding of succession in this country."

"Well then, let me let you in on a little secret." Franz leans into my space. I angle myself away but he whispers in my ear. "He's not the real deal. Not legitimate."

He leans back, probably to watch my reaction. I keep my face blank, and he continues, "Our mother liked a smorgasbord of men. Who knows who his real father is? It wasn't mine."

Behind my calm expression, my thoughts are racing back and forth, bumping into each other and falling down.

Franz pauses as if savoring the moment. "There's only one of us who has a chance at the throne, and it's not him."

"You're lying." I'm breathing hard. Franz has to be lying. This is crazy. Does Benedict know this? Does the queen know what is going on?

"One thing's true," Franz keeps talking. "Seduce two

brothers, you double your chances." I open my mouth to tell him off and he bends down, slanting his head to kiss my lips.

"Bleh!" I push him away and he grabs my arm.

Before he can do anything, Benedict's sharp voice interrupts. "Franz!"

Franz lets me go and I jump away from him. I wish I had a baseball bat handy. Is clobbering a royal an imprisonable offense? Probably. But it'd be worth it.

"Don't touch me," I say shakily.

Franz sneers at me but turns to his brother. Benedict blows past him, furious and sudden as a summer storm. He inserts himself between Franz and me, and puts his arm around my shoulders. He smells of popcorn, and I spot the tray with a full bowl of buttery goodness and two glass soda bottles on a side table.

He came to my rescue. I sag into him.

"Better watch her, brother," Franz snarls. "When she heard you're not headed to the throne, she was all too willing to ditch you for a short ride." It's such a lie, my face turns red and I can't speak.

"You will stay away from Frankie," Benedict commands. He steers me away, putting his back to his brother. "Did he hurt you?"

"No."

Behind us, Franz golf claps. "Good show. Eight out of ten." He mimes holding up a number like a judge. "French her, and you might convince me."

"I'm warning you," Benedict says, turning back around. "Leave her alone."

"So you're trying to tell me this is real?" Franz cocks his head to the side.

"My relationship with Frankie is none of your business," Benedict says and sneers. "Run along, boy. Go play with your toys. The grownups are talking now."

Franz flushes, and I know Benedict's jab hit its mark.

"She's a gold-digger," Franz shoots back, his hands fisted at his sides. "Everyone's talking about it. Why do you think the paparazzi is all over you? The story's about to break."

"Get out," Benedict thunders. His arm is rigid when I place a hand on it.

"It's okay, Benedict," I whisper. "He can't hurt me."

"But I can hurt him, Frankie," Franz says. "I know the truth. He's as fake as you are."

"What are you talking about?" I edge my tone with scorn. But Benedict stiffens at my side.

Franz can tell he's landed a blow. "That's right, big bro. I know your secret. You know, I always thought it was weird how perfect you acted all the time. Then I realized… you had to be. You're a bastard, in every sense of the word."

I wait for Benedict to deny it. The duke's jaw is clenched, his face paler than normal.

"And then I dug a bit deeper and figured out what this is." Franz waves a hand at both of us. "Another story. Another lie. People always compare me to you. Mr. Perfect. What would they say if they knew the truth?"

The silence between Franz's statements is heavy and awful.

"Don't worry, half-brother." Franz smirks over his shoulder as he turns away. "Your secret's safe with me." He pauses in the doorway. "For now."

"Get out," Benedict snaps, but Franz is already gone.

The silence after Franz has left is even more awful.

"Is it true?" I ask.

Benedict presses his lips together. For a long moment, I think he's not going to answer me. "Yes, it's true." He looks away. "It's the worst secret of my life. And if I'm not careful, it will destroy everything."

rankie

WE'RE ON THE LOVESEAT, curled up together. Franz is long gone. The movie is playing silently over our heads.

"I was twelve when I found out," Benedict says. "Overhearing an argument between my mother and the man I thought was my father. He always preferred Franz to me," he adds in a lower voice, almost as if he's talking to himself. "I always wondered why."

I squeeze his hand after a moment, bringing him back to me. "You must have been devastated."

His lips curve in a self-mocking grimace. "You should laugh at me. I was born with every avenue open to me. I was already in training to be Crown Prince—in case my aunt died and my mother became queen. Although, it was expected—not spoken of but hinted at—that my aunt would outlive my mother. My mother was wild even then. The details of my birth drove a wedge between her and her husband. The man I thought was my father. I always wondered why he was so cold…"

His mother and her husband were fighting the night she died, I remember with frozen clarity.

"What did you do?" I asked after he remained silent for a long while. "What did you do when you found out?"

He shakes himself, blinking like he's just been roused from a deep sleep. A reverie of memory. "I went along as normal, I suppose. Tried a little harder to be good. To be the best, to become the man they all needed me to be. After my mother died, my aunt brought me into a private audience. I was so nervous because it was her formal sitting room—the one where she speaks to presidents and prime ministers. Where she has her weekly debrief on the state of the nation. So I knew the meeting was serious. She told me the details of what I already knew: that my mother had lain with a man who was unmarried. There were hints of it in the paparazzi but she'd hidden it well enough. And I looked enough like Franz's father that the rumors were quelled. But if ever anyone went digging and found out… it would be the end of everything."

I bite my lip. I don't quite understand the importance of secession in this country, but to Benedict, it's everything. A duty. A destiny. A sword of Damocles hanging over his head.

"You've worked so hard," I murmur.

"Doesn't matter." He rubs his brow. "Franz knows. I suppose his father told him. I have enemies in the government. They would do anything to stop me from taking more power. If they found out I was a fraud—"

"You're not a fraud!" I shift to my knees to face him.

"Aren't I?"

"You're the best possible choice for Crown Prince; you

know that. Benedict," I cup his face, "you'd make a great king. You're amazing and responsible and… this country can't do better than you. You have my vote," I joke awkwardly.

He huffs. "I just don't know what else I can do. I've jumped through every hoop they've put me through. Like a trained show dog."

"So what does this mean? What would happen if your enemies found out?"

"They'd most certainly issue a challenge to my succession."

I bite my lip. I don't pretend to understand New Arcadia's complicated government, but I'll try for Benedict's sake. "What happens then? A duel, right? Can it be a schnitzel eating contest?" *Stop trying to joke, Frankie.*

"No." He sounds so tired. "Nowadays, it's a lawsuit. But even that is bad for the nation. Especially now. Once my aunt's pregnancy is announced, everyone will be waiting with bated breath to make sure she gives birth. Securing succession is of the utmost importance. Insecurity is bad for financial markets."

"God forbid the financial markets get their feelings hurt," I grumble under my breath.

That wins me a tired smile. But it drops away all too soon.

I can't fix this. I wish I could. "What can I do to help?"

"You are helping." He turns his head and kisses my palm, his five-o-clock shadow rasping on my skin. I shiver. He keeps kissing, moving to my wrist, up my arm. My heartbeat quickens. I shift to straddle his lap so he can reach more of me. "This," he murmurs against my skin. "I need this."

Yes. I can't change the facts but maybe I can make him feel better.

I let him kiss down my neck, to my collarbone, before

pushing him back and unbuttoning his shirt. This time he doesn't make a move to control me or my movements, and I take advantage of that. I spread my hands over his chest, admiring the muscles sprinkled with a few coarse dark hairs. "When do you even have time to work out?" I dip my head and kiss his collarbone. I kiss downward until I reach his belly, working at his belt at the same time.

He lets me take his cock out but tugs me upwards so I'm straddling him. With a firm grasp on my hips, he grinds me down over the hard length of him. I angle my hips so that it rubs the right spot, gasping as my arousal blooms in every corner of my body. My panties are wet. He rucks up my skirts, hooks his fingers in my underwear, and rips them off with a snap. I fall on him with a moan, my mouth slanting over his as he guides himself inside.

Even though I'm on top, he controls my movements with his hands on my hips. I rock over him, hungry for friction. His dick drags over my G-spot and I come, convulsing over him. After that, he makes me slow down, lifting me up and dipping himself carefully into my slick channel until I'm shuddering. I grab his shoulders, trying to force him to go faster, and he only slows his movements further like we're moving through honey.

"Come with me," he says against my mouth. He pumps his hips, slamming deep. My body tenses, and we gasp and go over together.

We lie against each other for a moment, panting. The light from the movie plays over Benedict's face. He looks relaxed, at peace.

"Frankie," he murmurs in the afterglow. His voice is full of meaning only I can understand. I've never felt so close, so intimate, with another person.

Later, we go to bed, and he falls straight to sleep. But I lie beside his slumbering form, staring into the velvety darkness.

Benedict told me his deepest, most wretched secret.

One day, I'll tell him mine.

CHAPTER 12

I WISH we could stay inside and make love all year, but the show must go on. On Monday, we hold a press conference to express our dismay at the trespassing photographer. Daniel words our statement cleverly, so we sound properly solicitous of the man's injury. On Tuesday, Benedict has a ribbon cutting for a new library. I'm photographed reading to the children. On Wednesday, we have more ceremonial duties, and make an appearance at a diplomat's dinner party. And so it goes.

Benedict and I spend a lot of time being cute together in public. In private, we say very little. Some cuddling. Light conversation. We don't mention Benedict's secret again.

On Friday night, I'm in the dressing room with the hair and make-up artist, getting ready for yet another ball.

I hear voices outside and straighten my slumped shoulders. One final spritz of hairspray, and the stylist pats my shoulder.

I turn to face the door just as Daniel opens it. He's wearing something only he could pull off—a sleek tux with an extra fancy cravat-like tie, secured with a brooch.

"Doing all right?" Daniel sweeps his keen gaze over me.

On cue, I curl my lips up. I'm tired of playing a polished, pore-less future duchess but I have to fake it.

"Oh, darling." He saunters into the room. He's holding a walking stick with a silver tip. The ornate metal matches the brooch. "You have to do better than that."

"I'll smile when I'm at the ball," I grumble, and smooth down my poufy pale blue princess dress. "How do I look?"

"Perfect," he says. "Except for one thing." He hands me a smooth white mask.

"A masquerade?" I ask, startled.

He steps behind me to fasten the ties. "Indeed."

Benedict swoops in, looking suave and handsome as usual. His black on black brocade mask hides the extra lines around his eyes that appeared this week. "You look lovely."

"Thank you. So do you." I glance at the mirror. The woman looking back at me is a stranger. I bite back a complaint—I wish I could stay home tonight, and rest. I touch my mask to straighten it and end up pushing it askew.

Daniel starts to move forward and Benedict holds up a hand.

"Allow me." He adjusts the mask carefully, and touches my lips. My lipstick is red as deadly berries.

"I've never been to a masquerade."

"We take off our masks at midnight," Daniel says.

"Do we ever really take off our masks?" I murmur. Both Daniel and Benedict raise a brow. The movement makes them look startlingly alike. One dark, one pale, but there's a similarity in their features. I'm not sure why I didn't notice it before.

"Are you all right?" Benedict asks in somber tone.

"Don't mind me." I wave a hand. I'm feeling especially fragile today. Brittle. Benedict shared himself with me, and it awoke something between us. Something beautiful and new. But raw.

I got a glimpse of Benedict, the man he is in private, but since our audience with the queen, he's back to being the duke.

The duke offers his arm. "Shall we?"

This week, we've played our parts with flawless protocol. The queen has announced her pregnancy, and this ball is to celebrate it. She'll be in attendance.

We have to be perfect, I remind myself as we sweep up the royal blue carpet and into the ballroom. Paparazzi and cameras line our route. Their cameras are little black gaping mouths, hungry for scandal. Waiting for us to fall so they can gobble us up. Or so I've been dreaming. I hope I'm not being overdramatic.

Daniel accompanies us, his dashing outfit completed by an ornate silver mask. He's coming in a capacity more than staff. Apparently he's a member of the nobility, too. His Ghanese father was related to the *Asantehene* or king of the Ashanti Empire, and when he traveled to New Arcadia to broker a trade treaty, he was given a New Arcadian royal title which Daniel inherited.

Tonight Benedict is on duty as part host, so Daniel keeps me company. I watch Benedict move around the room, greeting people. Even when Daniel and I waltz, I keep turning my head to follow the duke.

He leads a lady out onto the floor to dance with, and I sigh.

Daniel tilts his head. "Do your shoes hurt?"

"No." He knows very well I'm just tired.

"It's all right," Daniel murmurs. "You're doing well. There'll be the succession announcement and the coronation, and then Benedict will be busy and you can hide in the house. Eventually, you can quietly break up and fade into obscurity."

"And start classes at the university," I say. He nods. I watch Benedict dip his head to speak to his dance partner, a petite beauty with a fake Marilyn Monroe mole on her upper lip.

Once our pretend engagement is over, Benedict will be free to be with someone else. Date. Get engaged. Marry.

"It'll be over before you know it," Daniel assures me.

"Yes, I know," I reply brightly. I should be relieved to go back to my old life. It's not like I expected us to last. Everything we have is fake.

Daniel guides me into a series of complicated dance steps. I let him spin me around the ballroom and every time I stop, my eyes automatically search for Benedict.

At the end of the dance, there's pity in Daniel's eyes. "It'll all work out, Frankie, darling," he says. "Just don't fall in love."

Too late.

"Frankie," Benedict murmurs in my ear, and I turn. I stop myself before I do anything too dramatic—like fall into his arms.

"May I have this dance?" he asks.

"Of course," Daniel says for me, and hands me off.

Benedict and I fit closely together. His scent—crisp, with a hint of cologne—surrounds me as we swing into a classic waltz box step turn. We don't talk and don't look at each other. We don't need to. Our bodies speak in perfect harmony.

By the time the song ends, my tension has melted. Benedict guides me with a hand on my back, and even that feels right.

"Benny?" a woman's voice calls. "Benedict!"

Benedict frowns and turns slowly. I'm close enough to feel shock stiffen his body.

"Winnie," he says in a tired voice. For a second I don't place the name, then my head snaps around.

A buxom brunette in a small, diamond-studded mask sways up to Benedict. "It's so good to see you," she purrs, tugging her mask down. Winnie Bennett does look like me. Pale skin, long brown hair, maybe slightly taller. Her legs and arms and midriff are much thinner, but her boobs are as big as mine, and perky in a way that make me think they were enhanced surgically. Her lips are puffier than mine, too.

She smirks at me. "I see you wasted no time replacing me, Benny dear."

Benedict clears his throat and threads his arm around me. "This is my fiancée."

Winnie's eyes light with what looks like triumph. "Hello," she says to me coolly, without taking her gaze off Benedict. "I'm sure she won't mind if I claim a dance? For old time's sake?"

When he doesn't immediately deny her, I frown at Benedict. Winnie is acting way more familiar with my fiancé than I would expect her to.

But Benedict's expression is wooden, his eyes tired, and I realize it's all an act.

"Why, I don't mind at all," I return sweetly, with a touch of the Southern accent that Grandmère would lay on thick when she was being extra polite to someone she didn't like. "But *His Grace* and I were just about to go get refreshments." I emphasize *His Grace* to point out her appalling lack of manners, but Winnie doesn't seem to notice.

She pouts at us.

"Ah, there you are." Daniel magically appears at our side like a Victorian wizard, bless him.

"May I have this dance?" he says to Winnie, and takes her arm without waiting for an answer.

"And who are you?" She wrinkles her nose up at him, then realizes how handsome he is, and flutters her eyelashes.

Crisis averted.

Benedict touches my elbow, turning me to him. I start to congratulate him but I catch sight of a familiar figure beyond him, and freeze.

"Frankie?" The man from my nightmares stands not five feet away. Even with the mask, I recognize that superior drawl. He takes off his mask, and all my breath leaves my body. *It's him.* He's still tall, blond, with a cleft in his chin. Good looking in a bland, rich sort of way. Franz is right next to him, smirking at me.

"So the rumors are true," Chadwick says. There's amusement lurking in the corner of his mouth. Or possibly boredom. It's hard to tell with Chadwick Cawthorne the Fourth. Even when he was younger, his facial expressions had been frozen in a permanent smirk.

"Chadwick Cawthorne," Franz says, sweeping a hand out to usher him forward. "Let me introduce you to my brother, His Grace, the Duke of New Arcadia."

"We've met," Benedict says, his tone also balanced between bored and arrogant. His hand is still on my back, so he can probably tell I've turned to stone.

"Yes, but have you introduced Mr. Cawthorne to your new fiancée?" Franz asks.

"Fiancée?" Chadwick's smirk tips from condescending to aghast. "Frankie," he drawls in his nasal voice. Probably taking lessons in how to be condescending from his dad. "I must say, I didn't expect to see *you* here." He looks me up and down, still blinking, as if he's surprised I cleaned up and put on a dress. He only ever saw me in homemade cut-off jean shorts and a tank top—my hayseed summer uniform.

I clutch the skirts of my ball gown, the satiny fabric slipping through my fingers. I'm in full makeup, with my hair up in a complicated twist, and wearing a ten thousand dollar dress. Not typical armor, but armor just the same. *He can't hurt me.* Chadwick did his damage a long time ago.

"You're looking well," he says finally.

"Chadwick." My voice comes out hoarse.

Chadwick looks down his nose at me, at Benedict, at the room in general. "Actually, it's the Honorable Chadwick Cawthorne now. My father's just become a viscount." He inclines his head to the right, directing my gaze to the tableau behind him. A tableau straight from my nightmares.

His whole family is here, standing in a cluster, with Chad's parents in the middle. They stood in the same formation on that horrible summer afternoon I met them when I was seventeen. The first and last time I saw them. All the Cawthornes—from the snooty youngest to the eldest, pinch-faced Grand Dame—present for my humiliation.

Chadwick hadn't been there that day. As soon as his parents realized what he was doing with me, they shipped him off to a Swiss boarding school.

"Chadwick, darling." His mother glides forward. Her icy blue eyes and high cheekbones tell of good breeding, even if her skin is a little too pale. She's probably anemic from centuries of inbreeding—she looks a little like a half-made vampire. "Who is this?" She angles herself perfectly before us, her eyes on the duke. Waiting for an introduction.

Franz supplies it. "Lady Cawthorne, may I present my brother? And his fiancée." Her eyes barely glaze over me, dismissing me quickly. She's quick to do a half curtsy. No one here half curtseys to anyone except to the queen, but she's trying to get into the duke's good graces, I guess.

Benedict can tell that something is wrong with me. I'm stiff and silent by his side. But his good breeding kicks in, and he smoothly does a half bow that looks way more practiced and normal. "My lady, a pleasure to meet you." He also nods to the elder Chadwick Cawthorne, who has strolled over to stand beside his wife and son.

And I can't stop the memories from rushing back.

In a choked voice, I say, "Excuse me," and rush off, holding my baby blue skirts, like Cinderella fleeing at midnight.

It was bound to happen. I was hurtling to the moon. It was high time something made me crash.

I escape into the powder room and hide in a stall, sinking onto the toilet with my big skirts frothing around me. It's quiet in here, but for the faint lilting music from the live orchestra. No one else is in here. Daniel and I speculated that women fast and dehydrate themselves before entering a ballroom. From my experience, women only use the powder room to powder their noses and gossip. But at least I'm alone.

My gut churns, making me glad I haven't eaten or drunk anything. I rise and head out to the sinks, where I carefully dab water onto my chest. I look so different from the girl I was. There's no way Chadwick—stupid, self-absorbed man boy that he is—would have recognized me if he hadn't had Franz's help.

It was a set up. And it worked. I put my hand on my stomach, forcing myself to breathe. And the memory rises before me. Me, seventeen, out of my head in… love? Lust? Who even knows what those high strung teenage emotions are? The highs are ecstasy. The lows are agony. And logic and clear thinking are involved not at all.

He told me he loved me. He said it was forever. Now I know better. He was a bored rich kid, and he said what I wanted to hear so he could get into my pants. I wasn't his true love; I was a diversion. A way to pass a dull July.

But I'd thought it was real. A fairytale written in the stars. He was rich and handsome, if a little snooty. But my teen self had regarded his arrogance with awe. I was awkward and nervous, and he wanted to be with me anyway. He was my first, and it was perfect. Until I told him I'd missed my period.

He'd frowned, then kissed me softly. Fucked me one last time. And that was the last I ever saw of him—until now. When I'd gone the next day to find him in our usual secret hidden trysting place—an unused parlor the resort staff rarely cleaned—his mother had been waiting for me instead.

"Frankie," whines a voice, rudely cutting into my memories. My gaze is blurry. I have to wipe my eyes before I recognize who's interrupted my reverie—Winnie Bennett. My glamorous, vapid, possibly evil doppelganger. I didn't even hear her come in.

She has her hand on her hip. Cocks her head and looks me up and down much like Chadwick did earlier. Then she gives me a sneer.

"I don't know what he sees in you," she dismisses me, turning to admire herself in the mirror. "Other than me, of course. Total rebound material." She smirks at me in the mirror, then wipes away her lipstick and reapplies it. "You don't belong here."

You don't belong, you don't belong. The phrase echoes in my head. Did they teach it at boarding school in the Swiss Alps? Because Lady Cawthorne said that to me when I was seventeen, with exactly the same sneer, right before she told me her son would no longer be seeing me. I thought it was the worst moment of my life.

I was wrong. The worst came later.

My bodice is too tight. I back away, trying to breathe. I need air. I need to get out of here.

I run blindly out of the bathroom, not caring that Winnie Bennett is gloating. *She got what she came for tonight.*

I race out of the mansion. The night air hits me, carrying the scent of the river with it. I stagger across the lawn, skirts slipping from my hands. I'm getting grass stains on this beautiful satin but I don't care. I don't stop until I'm close enough to hear the water lapping against the bank.

I nearly drowned in this river a few balls ago. Someone shot fireworks at us. Maybe I should have taken it as a sign.

"Frankie," someone calls. It's Daniel. I wipe my face, glad that Benedict isn't here to witness this. He didn't come for me. He's probably inside, dancing with Winnie Bennett. *You don't belong here.*

Daniel arrives at my side. "What's wrong?" he asks and then sees my face. "Come, darling." He holds out his arm. "We'll get you home."

I hope he's using the royal 'we', and I can slink home with no one besides Daniel noticing, but Benedict meets us at the car. Daniel passes me to him. Before I can protest, Benedict's arms are around me. He tucks his jacket around my shoulders and bundles me into the car.

In the darkness, I scoot away, but he follows me and I let him cradle me. The car rolls past Daniel, illuminating his worried face, before heading on into the night.

"I'm sorry," I croak, but Benedict hushes me. He palms my cheek and presses me to his shoulder. "Later. We'll talk later."

rankie

"ALL RIGHT," Benedict says once I'm showered and dressed in comfortable clothes, back in Lady Ursaline's manor. I'm safely ensconced on a couch with a glass of scotch in my hand. I take a sip and grimace, handing the half full glass to him. He downs it in one swallow and sets it aside. Instead of taking a seat next to me on the couch, he lifts me up and sits back down with me in his lap. "Tell me what happened."

"I should've told you from the start." I can't look at him. I'm grateful the room is dark, a few lamps offering pools of light that don't touch the greater gloom. Fitting for this conversation. "I never thought it would come out. If I had—"

"Shh, Frankie. I know."

"There was a boy," I start slowly, "and I thought I knew what I was doing. I'd watched so many movies, so many fairy tales." I choke up for a moment, wishing I didn't sound so pathetic. "I thought that I knew the script. But reality isn't a fairytale. Happy endings aren't real." I stare into Benedict's dark eyes, wishing I could telepathically communicate the rest.

"Did he…" Benedict's face tightens.

"No," I say quickly. "It was all consensual. I was seventeen."

"He was older—" Benedict starts, but I cut him off with a shake of my head.

"The age of consent in my state is sixteen. And it was consensual."

"But he was older," Benedict repeats. "He knew better."

I shrug. "His family came to the resort. My mother and father worked there. It was summer, and I was left to my own devices. I was old enough to take care of myself. I was supposed to stay at Grandmère's house, but it was hot and stuffy. So I snuck up to the resort to meet the rich kids. And that's how I met Chad." I'd felt so fancy in my dollar store sunglasses. The girls laughed at me, but Chadwick talked to me. As soon as I learned his name, I should have known he'd be a dick.

"He said he would take care of me," I explain haltingly. "I assumed that meant to marry me and love me forever. And then…" I suck in a breath and say the rest in a rush. "I missed my period—I'd never done that before—and told him. When I went back the next day, he was gone. His mother pulled me into this sitting room where the Cawthorne family had all assembled. They made it clear that gold-diggers weren't to be tolerated. I guess I was a lesson to the younger kids." I wipe the wet off my cheeks.

The room is still and quiet as a tomb. "What about your period?" Benedict asks gently. He's really being too good.

"Chadwick must have told his parents. Mrs. Cawthorne had me go into a small side room where they'd arranged to have a private doctor administer a pregnancy test. Luckily, it was negative. Mrs. Cawthorne watched over me the whole time." I look down at my hands. "I think… I think that if it had been positive, the doctor would've done more. It was so humiliating," I end on a whisper.

Benedict rubs my back slowly. I have to get through this.

"When it was clear I wasn't pregnant, Chadwick's mom handed me an envelope of money."

For your silence, she'd said. *I assume your parents don't know about this, nor their employers. I suggest we keep it that way. Better for all involved.*

"I knew then that she would complain. My parents would lose their jobs, which meant they wouldn't be able to pay their mortgage. The resort was the biggest employer in town. So I went home; packed a bag. I put up an ad saying I was a pet sitter and willing to travel. I had graduated high school early, and was just trying to figure out how to save up enough for college. I told my parents that I wanted to travel. I completely lied to everybody." I cover my face. "I'm sorry." I wish I wasn't sitting on Benedict's lap. "I should just go—"

"No, darling. I'm sorry. I'm so sorry you went through that. The way those people treated you… no wonder you hated me."

"No. I didn't hate you."

"Didn't trust me, then."

"Maybe."

He keeps rubbing my back.

"So now you know my secret. I never thought it would blow up like this. I didn't know they would be here in New Arcadia, I didn't know—"

"Shhh, Frankie." He stops my word torrent with his fingers, then his lips. A light kiss, there and gone. "We'll figure it out."

"No." I feel numb, and so tired. "I can't do it anymore. Don't you see? They're going to call me a gold-digger again.

They'll use this to tear you down. The scandal will be huge. I can't do this."

"I can protect you," he says, and I want to believe him.

"But is it worth it?"

"Yes." He tips my chin up. "Frankie, you're worth it."

"No. It's not going to work. We're just delaying the inevitable."

"The way I see it, there's a way to fix this." He shifts me off his lap onto the couch, and tucks the blanket around me.

Then he gets down on one knee.

I shoot up straight in my seat. "Benedict," I say in alarm. "What are you doing?"

"What I should have done in the first place. Darling…" He takes my hand. "I know it's unconventional…"

He's proposing for real. This isn't the way this conversation needs to go. I start to mutter under my breath, "No, no, no—"

"Shhh. Please. I know it's been hard. I know you're scared. But we have something here. Something real. And I… I want more."

"Benedict." He's not thinking with his head. He's as lost in this farce as I am. I have to wake him up, make him see. *It's fake.*

"Frankie." His thumb strokes over my knuckles. "Let me protect you. Make me the happiest man in the world. As my duchess, you'll belong anywhere."

Tempting. So tempting.

You think you could ascend to our set? Mrs. Cawthorne had hissed. *You will never be good enough. You will never be one of us.* She'd thrown the envelope at my feet. *Take the money, and go. Don't let us catch you around here again.*

I could marry Benedict. I could pretend this theater is real. We're not acting anymore. Our feelings have changed. But feelings fade. Chad's did.

In one year, when Benedict wakes up from the fairytale, will he forgive me? Or will he resent me forever?

I swallow around the mountain-sized boulder in my throat. "And then what?" I prompt him to think it through.

"We move in together for real."

I make a show of looking around at this room—one of many in the manor's wing Lady Ursaline gave over to our use. "Face the paparazzi and the Cawthornes together?" We've run from both of them in the span of a week. But that's not the biggest problem. Benedict grimaces and opens his mouth, but I grip his hands tighter and lean forward. "It's not them that's the problem, is it? It's the queen's cabinet. They don't want you to become king or crown prince."

He leans back, nostrils flaring. That punch landed.

"This isn't going to work," I say slowly. I knew this relationship was fake. I knew it would end. So why do I sound so heartbroken? "You can't protect me. Not from this. The scandal will get bigger and bigger, and eventually they'll pull out bigger guns. They'll find out the truth of your birth. It'll be everywhere." I pull my hands out from his and paint an imaginary headline. "*Crown Prince, a bastard in every way.*"

The lines of his shoulders turn to stone. I hate not pulling my punches, but he's not being sensible.

"They'll call you a fraud," I say. "And even if they don't, the wrong people will find out and hold it over your head forever."

He blinks and glances away, and I know I have him. I cup his beautiful face in my hands, lifting his head to mine as his stubble scratches my palms.

This is the death blow. Dagger to the heart. And I have to make sure it goes all the way in.

"Fairytales aren't real. This relationship isn't real. It means nothing. Not compared to everything you've worked for."

"No," he says, and he sounds just as broken as I do.

"The crown, Benedict. Eye on the prize." He means too much to his country. I won't let him let them down.

"No," he growls. "I won't allow it." He rips my blanket away and surges forward, pushing me back on the couch. He guides me down and stretches over me, his hand already slipping my sweatpants down. I reach for him, too, sliding my hands under his soft t-shirt to stroke the flexing muscles underneath. He frees his cock and finds my entrance, gliding into me with only a few pauses to let me adjust to his size. I run my nails over his lower back and further down, where I cup his taut buttocks. I can't deny the way we fit together.

Benedict hunches to kiss me, his lips wild. He fucks me deep into the couch, as if he would imprint his possession on my body. He rages over me, and I'm quickly caught up in his passion. Licking, scratching, even biting as we writhe together, two bodies pressed and joined together, intent on becoming one.

"Frankie." He grips my hair, tugging my head back. I meet his feral eyes. "Come with me," he orders, with a sharp yank that sends a bite of pain singing through my scalp. The sting is swallowed immediately by the bliss growing in my body. "Come now," he commands.

I do, my whole body seized and consumed by pleasure. He pumps himself into me, holding my eyes, then swallows my cry with his kiss.

We lie together, pressed chest to toe on the couch. He shifts to his side but keeps his body half covering mine. And I'm grateful for the weight.

But even as he falls asleep, his face tucked between my neck and shoulder, I know the truth. His scent mingled with mine, the soreness where he stretches me, the marks on my body from his rough kisses—they won't stay.

We have this night. We might have tomorrow.

But we don't belong together. I don't belong with him. *I don't belong.*

Winnie Bennett and Viscountess Cawthorne were right.

* * *

Frankie

WHEN I WAKE up the next morning, Benedict is gone. He left a note in perfect cursive saying he'll be back for lunch. I make my way to the dining room, where we've been taking our meals. Daniel is waiting there.

"Sleep well?" he asks softly.

I shrug and head to the sideboard. Instead of the usual array of newspapers beside the franzbrötchen and pudding-bretzel, there's only the Financial Times.

"Where are the papers?" I demand, turning to Daniel.

He looks uneasy.

"I can always go out and buy one."

"Not if you don't want to start a riot," he says, and I wince.

"That bad?"

He sighs and pulls a stack out of his smart leather satchel. I wait until he's spread them out and then approach them all at once.

It's bad. Very bad. The scandal equivalent of a nuclear meltdown. My face and Benedict's are plastered on every front page. Sometimes Chadwick's headshot dances between pictures of the two of us.

According to the more respectable papers, I'm a social climber with 'provincial roots'. According to the more sensational ones like 'Redux' and 'The Daily Knot', I'm a money-grubbing whore, and possibly an American spy seducing powerful men for their secrets. There's no direct quote from Chadwick, but his father, Lord Cawthorne, made a statement: *We stand in support of Her Majesty and her government. We have no association with Ms. Beaumonde, nor do we wish one in the future.* Brief but vague—but any opinion from a newly minted Viscount holds weight.

The real damning stuff is the statement by Franz: *My brother is a smart man. Too smart to fall for someone like her.* One column quoted someone who speculated that our relationship was a publicity stunt, but mostly, the reporting seemed to waver between casting Benedict as a cold diplomat finally brought low, or a poor sod who was fooled by a pretty face and a 'generous rack'.

"We'll file lawsuits," Daniel says smoothly. "Libel, slander."

I rub my forehead. "Won't that make it worse? Stir up more scandal?"

"Frankie," he takes my hand and tugs me away from the papers, "there's no way to stir up more scandal. We've hit the max."

Not if someone digs out Benedict's secret. I bite my lip to keep from blurting this out. Daniel probably knows about Benedict's bastardy.

"This is awful," I whisper. "This is the worst possible thing that could happen." I pull my hand out of Daniel's gentle grip. He's trying to soothe me; I don't deserve to be soothed. "This is the opposite of what you wanted. I was supposed to help!"

"You did help. Frankie, this is a fluke. The paparazzi loved you."

"Until they didn't."

"Well, yes."

"I should've told you about Chadwick. I honestly didn't think it would come up. I've never told anyone about what happened. Not even my family. Only Benedict, last night."

"I understand," Daniel says gently. But he deserves to

know the full story, so I give him an abbreviated version. When I'm done, his dark eyes glitter.

"You should have told us. Not because of the scandal. But so we would stand by you. Frankie," he catches my shoulders to turn me towards him, "we stand by you."

"Thank you." I collapse in his arms, getting a hug I didn't know I needed.

"Of course," he murmurs. "We care about you. We could have made plans to publicly shun the Cawthornes."

I stiffen, and he squeezes me tighter before letting me loose and adding, "Benedict still might"

I rub my arms as I step away from Daniel, suddenly cold. Benedict, Chadwick, the Cawthornes, Franz—it's all such a mess. I can't get my head around it.

"So what now?" I hope Daniel has a plan.

"Now we wait. Benedict was called to the palace. An early audience with the queen."

I bite my lip. That's bad.

"Chin up, Frankie." Daniel doesn't leave it to chance—he reaches out and lifts my chin with a finger. "It might not be so bad."

I bite my lip, and nod. I fake a small smile—but neither Daniel nor I are fooled.

* * *

BENEDICT

I'm waiting in a green room adjacent to the queen's main parlor, awaiting an audience with her. My aunt is closeted with her cabinet and closest advisors. They were scheduled to meet anyway for budgetary concerns, and planning to make the line of succession official. It's just bad luck this scandal broke this morning.

Last night, I woke in the wee hours and couldn't get back to sleep. I carried Frankie to our bed—we'd passed out on the couch after our glorious fuck—and sat for hours in the grey gloom, watching her sleep.

I didn't need to read the papers this morning to know how bad it would be. Daniel will do his best to mitigate the worst, but a crossroads is becoming increasingly clear:

Give up Frankie, or lose everything. Let down the queen, my aunt, and my entire country.

I rub my forehead, then glance at the two palace guards guarding the door. I smooth my suit, trying for some composure. The air in the palace is heavier today.

The sound of scraping chairs tells me it won't be long now.

"Excuse me a moment, gentlemen," my aunt's cultured voice carries through the door.

One of the guards opens the door in anticipation and a few seconds later the queen walks through.

"Benedict," she says. Her skin looks papery and pale, her eyes tired. It's on the tip of my tongue to ask her how she's feeling, and invite her to sit.

Instead, I bow and wait for the blow.

"I trust you know why I called you here this morning?"

"Yes, ma'am."

She tilts her head back to the room she just left. "They've spent the morning telling me this is proof you're unfit to lead."

The breath leaves my body. This is it.

My aunt's shoulders wilt. Her aura of power slips for a moment, leaving nothing but a petite, forty-something woman with a worn expression. "They still don't know, Benedict. Oh, a few of them might guess. But your secret is safe. For now." Her voice hardens. "I told you to fix it. I trust in your ability to shoulder responsibility. To do your duty." She fixes me with a gimlet stare. "Can I count on you?"

There's a lump of coal in my throat. I swallow and nod. "I'll fix it."

The queen continues to stare at me for a long moment, then shakes her head and swans past me, heading back to her advisors. "See that you do."

* * *

Frankie

"You never told me," Mina says. I'm sitting in one of the manor's many parlors, on the couch with my laptop in front of me and my legs tucked up under a duvet. "I always wondered why you left home so young and never really went back."

Benedict is still in audience with the queen. Daniel had to leave to run interference with the press, but not before making sure I felt supported. He encouraged me to talk to someone trustworthy about everything—he even offered a therapist, which I declined. Instead, I promised to reach out to Mina. To prove it, I set up my laptop and messaged her right in front of him. Even with the time difference, she was awake—probably never went to sleep.

Daniel was right. Sharing my secret shame with trusted friends did make me feel better. I wish I hadn't waited so long.

"I think," I say slowly, still turning my reasons over in my head, "I was sure the Cawthornes would get my parents fired. My folks worked at the resort for years—it was the biggest employer in town. If they lost their jobs, they'd prob-ably lose our house." I shrug, and grab a tissue to blow my nose. I've already cried a few tears, now I'm feeling more calm. "I was young; I didn't know what else to do."

Mina's silent for a second. Then she growls, "I want to destroy these motherfuckers. Starting with Douchey McDouche face."

"No, it's all right." I wave the tissue. "Please don't."

"Are you sure? Cawthorne Holdings might be worth billions, but I bet their computer security is crap. I can sneak in, find their vulnerabilities. Create a zero day exploit and sell it to the highest bidder…" She's typing on her computer now, so fast, it sounds like her fingers are crashing on the keys.

I wrinkle my nose. "I don't know what that means but it sounds bad."

"It is." She stops typing for a moment and looks straight into the camera. Her grin would make a shark swim in the opposite direction. "We could topple their entire business, and make a fortune."

"No." I sit up. "Nothing illegal.'"

"It's only illegal if we get caught," she singsongs.

"Absolutely not. Mina," I say in a firm tone, channeling my inner duchess. "I don't want you risking anything for me. Besides," I add in a softer voice, "I don't want to spend another second thinking about that family."

"Fair enough. But the offer stands."

The murmur of deep voices just outside the door catches my attention. Benedict's back, for better or worse.

"I have to go." I blow Mina a kiss. The call ends and I close my laptop, setting it aside. I haven't dressed up for my day yet.

When I step out into the hall, only Daniel's there. I have to call his name twice before he answers. His fists and jaw are clenched.

"Daniel?" I approach with caution. "Where's Benedict?"

"His Royal Arrogance is in the study," Daniel grits out. "You can go in when you're ready."

I move past him, but on impulse, I put my hand on Daniel's rigid arm. "It'll be okay." My heart is sinking but my voice is steady.

After a second he sighs and shakes his head. "I told him we could find another way. If he's not willing to fight for you at least as hard as he's fought for the throne then he doesn't deserve—"

I raise a hand to stop the torrent. "Don't be hard on him, Daniel. He was raised this way."

"That's no excuse."

"Not for someone like Chadwick. But Benedict's trying to do the honorable thing. Besides, things were clear from the beginning. This was always meant to come to an end."

Daniel's shoulders lower an inch. "I suppose. We'll take care of you, Frankie. As far as I'm concerned, you upheld your end of the deal."

I hold back a snort. "We both know I made things worse."

"Yes, well," he glares at the closed door to the room Benedict's using as his study, "I won't abandon you." *Unlike him,* is his unspoken addition.

"It was fun while it lasted." On impulse, I pop up on tiptoe and kiss Daniel's cheek. "Time to exit stage right."

He watches me sadly as I go into Benedict's study and close the door.

The only light is from the window. Benedict stands in front of it, his large form framed by the dark curtains.

This is it. The final act.

I open my mouth and try to remember my lines.

"I know it's time for me to go. I'll coordinate with Daniel in case you need anything else from me." I run out of words, and Benedict still hasn't turned around. Maybe it's too painful for him.

I know this is for the best. I know our relationship was all an act. If there was a moment I thought I could play the part perfectly enough to make it real, I was only fooling myself. In another life, we might belong together. What I told Daniel was true—I had fun. It was a game, and I enjoyed some of it: sparring with Lady Ursaline, fooling dignitaries, and seducing Benedict.

I'll miss those things. But most of all, I'll miss being with Benedict. Not His Grace. Not the Minister of Finance or future Crown Prince. Just Benedict.

But at least I got the chance to be with him, even for a little while.

"Thank you," I say. "For everything."

The duke's shoulders are strong and square, filling the window frame. I wait another minute and then nod to no one. He's not going to turn around. Maybe it's his way of making things easy. Sucking all his emotion inside so he can do his duty.

It hurts my heart, but it's not my place to help anymore.

My hand is on the door handle when I hear him say, "If I could change things, I would." His voice is rough and low.

But he doesn't say any more, and he doesn't turn around.

"Goodbye, your Grace," I murmur, and leave.

CHAPTER 14

enedict

THE PRESS CONFERENCE in which Daniel announces my break up with Frankie was brief. It went well, I'm told. I wanted to do it, but Daniel said this was better. My next appearance in public should be focused on new initiatives from the Ministry of Finance. Focus on playing the part of a responsible leader for this country. I didn't realize how much I was faking until Frankie entered my life and turned it upside down. Like a movie in black and white flipped to technicolor —I didn't know what I was missing until I had more.

And now it's gone. Frankie is gone. And there's a hollow in my chest where my heart used to be.

Two weeks later, I'm in attendance to the queen, along with all her indispensable advisors, and a host of dispensable ones. The throne room is packed with nobles arranged in order of importance, the greatest to least. I'm up near the front, close to the throne.

175

Today the queen announces her successor. Her advisors aren't a hundred percent on my side, but enough of them are convinced I'll be able to steer the country well if the queen dies or takes an absence. Ending my engagement helped.

The tabloid frenzy has also died down somewhat. It helped that Franz wrecked his brand new red Lamborghini Aventador in a 300-year-old Baroque fountain two days ago. Of course my idiot brother emerged without a scratch, but the spectacular accident has dominated the news cycles, followed closely by my breakup with so called 'gold-digger', Francis Beaumonde.

I've filed lawsuits against the worst of the papers, but Daniel says I don't have enough political capital to do much more than that. Freedom of speech is important, but there are a few editors I wish I could challenge to a duel.

My jaw aches from gritting my teeth. I know I've lost weight. But I'm so close. I'll put on a game face. Fake it. Get through this royal audience, and then the press conference scheduled immediately afterwards. And the next. And the next.

The show must go on.

The Cawthornes are present, their smug faces arranged in a row across from me. They're up near the front, too, skipping in line ahead of titles five centuries older than theirs, simply because they're wealthy, and their companies add a fifth of a percent to our GDP.

The eldest Cawthorne—the Viscount—reached out to me, offering vague sympathy for my recent break-up, and offering his support. *I hope we can work together in the future to strengthen trade for our great nation.* I can read between the lines as well as the next duke. Any offer of support is a trap. He'd expect *quid pro quo,* and more.

Daniel didn't let me send a response. He also won't allow

me to levy revenge against the Cawthornes. Too bad. I've thought up seventy-six different ways to destroy their political, social and financial standing. Only three are illegal.

I stay up at night, plotting them. Ignoring the side of the bed where Frankie slept, the handful of nights we were together.

Daniel says my mood's been particularly awful since the break-up. The arrogance turned cruel. He blames it on my lack of sleep, but we both know better. Frankie's gone and with her, my reasons, my desire to be better. My sharp edges are all I have left.

I never suffered fools gladly but lately, I don't suffer them at all.

An advisor to the queen is droning on about precedent or some such nonsense. Typically I'd be paying attention to every detail, but I can't seem to focus.

I wish Frankie was here. Not that fiancées are generally invited to this sort of meeting, but if she were here, she would make it fun. She'd watch everything with a beautiful docile expression and then turn her face so that only I could see her, and wrinkle her nose.

She'd whisper some quip about how Sir Charles looks like Santa Claus's thinner younger brother. Or how Mr. Green would be her top suspect in a murder investigation. Something wacky and wonderful. *Mr. Green in the throne room with the garrote.* She'd waggle her dark brows. *Or was it the guillotine?* And she'd smile.

And then I'd get hard, and spend the rest of the assembly pondering how to sneak to an unused room and fuck her senseless on an antique brocade chair.

But Frankie's gone. And all my fun went with her. My life stretches in front of me a long chain of endless meetings. As Crown Prince, I'll have even more responsibilities. Responsibilities I've prepared for all my life—but why? For what? What is it all for?

Frankie's face comes to mind. But she's gone, and I can't have her.

The queen raises a finger, summoning me. I nod and make my way to her side.

In a minute, the queen is going to declare me her official heir. I look out over the sea of prune-faced nobles, hanging on the queen's every word. Sycophants. They'd stab me in the back and wipe their shoes on my fallen body on their way to more power.

Is this what I wanted?

I'm a fraud. Everything about my life is fake. Frankie was the only thing that was real, and I let her go.

"And now we're pleased to make the next announcement," my aunt says.

"No," I blurt out and she startles, her head whipping around to me.

"Benedict?" Her eyebrow arches, wrinkling her forehead.

My whole life depends on what I say next. How much should I sacrifice for love? My position? My standing? My whole kingdom?

Frankie didn't think she was worth it, but she was wrong. She's worth this. She's worth everything.

I lean down so my lips are level with the queen's ear. "I'm sorry. I'll support you in any way I can. But I can't do this anymore."

And I turn to face the room.

"I have an announcement to make." There's a giddy rush like I'm standing on the edge of a cliff, then I leap. "I'm a bastard."

Dead silence. It stretches on for a few seconds, then someone mutters, "Well, we knew that." It's a joke, but no one laughs.

I clear my throat. "I'm illegitimate," I clarify. "I cannot inherit the throne." I pause a moment to let that sink in, and then project my voice over the growing murmurs. "Not unless you overturn the laws. Even if you did, I'm not sure I want it. I prefer my post in the Ministry of Finance. And I intend to support Her Majesty's decrees. I love this country, and I wish to serve, but I can't live this lie any longer."

Loud arguments break out in the room as I straighten and walk off, heading down the red carpet towards the back of the room, near the windows. The nosebleed section, where I belong.

My arms swing easily as I go. A great weight has tumbled from my shoulders. I float along, enjoying the lack of pressure. From the sounds behind me, the cabinet members have surrounded the throne, already in full discussion. I don't look back.

I pass Mr. Cawthorne, who looks like he's sucked a lemon. My enemies have nothing on me, I realize with a dizzy wave. They aren't going to get what they want.

I stop at the end of the room and look down onto the rose garden below. The press is waiting beyond them for their invitation inside. Daniel is out there. He's going to be relieved and pissed at me in equal measure.

I can't wait to tell Frankie.

"Well," drawls a nasal voice. "That was unexpected." Chadwick Cawthorne approaches me, hands in his pockets. He sidles up and surveys the rose garden below. "My father was wondering how you'd handle it. Didn't think you'd have the balls to come clean."

I blink, unable to believe what I'm hearing.

The billionaire viscount's son seems all too willing to overshare. "He told me if the Winnie Bennett scandal didn't work out, he had something else to hang over your head." I turn slowly, blood beating a battle rhythm in my ears.

Chad shrugs. "But you just gave it all up."

The advisors thronging around the throne are getting louder. I glance back to see if the queen's okay. My aunt looks tired, slouched in her grand chair with two fingers pressed to her temples. My great aunt Ursaline elbows her way into the fray, standing between the queen and the members of cabinet most likely to spit when upset. Lady Ursaline catches me watching and gives me a big wink.

That's all right then. I turn back to the window and decide I don't want to be near Chadwick anymore. He's still talking.

"I never would have thought you'd throw everything over." He shrugs. "I guess being king probably wouldn't be all that it's cracked up to be."

"What do you want?" I ask.

He raises a brow. "Oh, father would like us to get into bed together." He laughs at his crude expression and waves a hand. "In the business sense, of course. He wants first pick of all building contracts. He knows you chose where to direct funds for all infrastructure projects. Of course I told my dad you and I are already *lochschwagers*."

I translate the German word as *wiener brothers* but say nothing, mostly because I can't quite believe someone would use that word.

Chadwick takes my silence to mean I don't understand. "Ya know? Dipped our wicks into the same hole." He elbows me.

Red lights flash behind my eyes. I take a step back. "I beg your pardon." My tone could freeze hot coals.

"She's a great lay," Chadwick continues, blithely unaware of my growing ire. "Pity she's a social climbing whore who—"

But I never find out the rest of that sentence. As soon as he says the words *social climbing*, my arm swings back of its own volition and thwacks Chadwick a good one, right in the face.

He staggers back, blood blooming in the corner of his mouth. My fist throbs. The pain feels amazing.

"What the fuck?" His shout draws attention from the rest of the room. He touches his mouth and his fingers come away red.

"Chadwick!" His father calls his son to heel but Cawthorne the Lesser is not listening.

"Oh, you fucking asshole. You're going to pay for that." He launches himself at me.

"What ho, fisticuffs!" Lady Ursaline shouts with glee. There's a scrape of chairs as people move out of our way.

I launch myself at Chad again. I try to get another punch in but he blocks his face. Of course. He's too pretty to take a punch there. I land one in his gut and send him reeling backwards, gasping like a banked carp.

"Chadwick," his father snaps. The viscount heads for us but someone pulls him back.

"Was she a great fuck, Benny?" Chadwick snarls. "Or did she lie still under you and think of *me*?"

I wade in again but this time he gets a few punches in.

"Bastard," he hisses.

"That's right," I growl back. And something in me snaps. *My secret's out.* My duty done. I don't have to be perfect any longer.

My next punch sends Chad reeling. I follow it up with an inept attempt to knee his groin. It hits his thigh instead and he staggers. He comes at me again, fists flailing.

"Where did they teach you that?" I sneer, giving him a taste of his own condescension. "Swiss boarding school?"

Chadwick howls, and rushes at me. I step swiftly out of the way.

I may have grabbed the back of his coat and sent him

flying farther than momentum would carry him. Or maybe the thin panes of glass in the large windows should have been replaced two centuries ago. Either way, Chadwick flies head first into the window and crashes through the glass. His cry echoes as he falls.

Several nobles rush to the broken window.

I pop my cuffs and straighten my torn coat. "He'll be fine," I tell the hushed room. "The rose bushes will have broken his fall." And I turn on my heel and stride to the door.

Franz is there, entering. Late as usual, and looking more sheepish than usual. Probably bracing himself for a dressing down about his latest scandal.

I allow myself a brief smile. The cabinet might not want a bastard, but they'll be tearing at their hairpieces within the first five minutes of dealing with Franz.

My half-brother's head snaps up when he sees me. My tie's askew, my coat is torn, and there's blood trickling from the edge of my mouth. His jaw drops towards his feet.

I grip his shoulder briefly and pull him into a brutal hug that's half chokehold. "You want the throne so much? It's yours." He staggers when I release him, but a few guards reach out to steady him. I stride on.

"Benedict, Benedict!" someone calls after me. I pretend not to hear, but pause before rounding the corner when the queen asks, "But where is he going?"

"To fetch Frankie," Lady Ursaline booms a reply.

"Who?" The queen sounds bewildered.

There's satisfaction in Lady Ursaline's bellowed response. "His duchess."

* * *

Frankie

. . .

"I'VE DECIDED to count my blessings," I tell Elvis. "For example: I could have actually been pregnant and forced to get an abortion." I shudder. "I could have been a tad less intimidated by Mrs. Cawthorne and told everyone what happened, and my parents would have lost their jobs. And I never would have taken up pet sitting and met you." I scratch the back of Elvis's neck the way he likes it. He bows his head so I can reach his itchy spots better. "And I never would have met Benedict," I add softly. Like it or not, that goes firmly in the *I do not regret* column. Because I don't regret meeting the duke. His Grace. Dukey McDuke face, as Mina now calls him to make me laugh. My time with Benedict was wonderful. He wasn't meant to be. But it certainly showed me how perfect a man can be even if he has the world on a platter and a whole cabinet full of silver spoons.

"My Grandmère called the other day," I continue to share. Elvis has proved a great therapist, these past weeks. "I told her the whole story. She cried. And so did my parents—I told them, too. I'm going home to visit next Christmas." Elvis shakes his feathers, and fluff poofs out in a cloud. "No, I won't leave you. I'm still going to university here—Daniel got me permission to take the first two semesters online. And when I'm done with this job, I'll ask Lady Drey if I can come visit. I think she'll take pity on me when I tell her you're my second best friend." I think she'll understand.

I hold out my hand and Elvis hops on, stepping sideways up my arm and clawing up to sit on my shoulder. "Who shall we watch today? Cary Grant, or Jimmy Stewart?"

"Give it to me, big boy," Elvis chirps.

"Philadelphia Story it is." Another day, another movie marathon. It's a lonely little life, but it's mine.

The doorbell rings right before a drunk Tracy Lord tells everyone she has feet of clay. I turn up the volume. Whoever rang the doorbell will go away.

But it rings again.

"Go away," I shout. There's more doorbell ringing, and then knocking. I leave Elvis watching the movie and head to the front door to check the peephole. It's Daniel, in white jeans, white boots, a white-faced watch, and a white shirt under a silky orange jacket. He looks ready for a photo shoot.

I push back my messy hair. I haven't bothered to brush it for a few days. My eyes might be a little red from my last crying jag.

Whatever. I open the door.

"There you are." Daniel looks me up and down. "Miss Havisham."

"Bite me." I go to close the door, and he stops it with his elegant boot. So I back up and let him in. We stand awkwardly facing each other in the foyer. He reaches out and pushes back a tendril of my hair.

"I told you not to fall in love with him," he says gently.

I shake my head, looking away only to have my eyes snap back when he adds, "I would have been wrong."

"No," I say, and even to my own ears, I sound defeated. "You were right."

"It's better to have loved and lost..." Daniel quotes.

"Bullshit."

He laughs and pulls me into a hug. Despite myself, I relax against him. It feels good. I haven't had a hug since before the break-up.

"Are you here to check if I'm still alive?"

"Something like that." He ends the hug and salutes Sir Fred in the corner. "Have you left the house since..."

I press my lips together and shake my head.

"I thought so. Come now, Lady Misery. Let me take you out."

"Why?" I ask.

"Because it's time. There's a movie playing in the park. Fireworks after." Two brown fingers stop my protest. "Elvis will be okay for a few hours."

I nod because Daniel's right. What the heck. It's time for me to start living my life. Even if I really don't want to.

rankie

MY FIRST SURPRISE comes when we pull into the park. "Here?" I ask. There's the outdoor theater Benedict and I passed the time we fled the paparazzi.

"New public initiative. Summer movie nights in the park." He tugs my hand. I duck my head as we pass people, but I'm in disguise. Daniel waited for me to dress, then he did my hair, and handed me a pair of huge sunglasses and a head-scarf. I look like Sofia Loren.

But that doesn't stop someone from recognizing me. "Over here!" A young Latina woman with a big grin waves from the front row. She looks familiar.

I pull off my sunglasses. "Mina? What are you doing here?"

My internet friend rises. She's smaller than I realized—petite, and curvy. I've never met her in person.

"Somebody invited me out." She winks at Daniel. "I

figured it's time for me to come and meet you in person." She turns to Daniel and explains, "I'm her best friend. Mostly because I'm her only friend."

"You are not my only friend." I laugh even though she's right.

"Elvis doesn't count." Mina waggles a finger at me.

"I'm her friend too," Daniel says in a hurt tone.

"Yes, you are." I'm glad that losing Benedict didn't mean I lost Daniel.

"Shall we?" Mina motions to two empty seats next to hers. She must have saved them, because the rest of the theater is filling up. The sun is setting, but people are still wandering about the park, strolling with friends or walking their dogs. There's a game of frisbee in a nearby field. On the hill behind the formal seating, people are spreading blankets out and picnicking.

"I thought that this would be a great place to have old movies nights," I whispered to Mina.

"So you did," says Daniel. "Maybe someone paid attention."

I peer at him, but he smiles at the stage in front of us and doesn't elaborate.

"Does anyone else smell popcorn?" Mina asks.

"Yes." Daniel rises. "I'll get it. Stay here and catch up."

I turn my frown to Mina. "What are you two up to?"

"Nothing." She blinks, all innocence, but she can't stop grinning. "Just remember, it's not over until the fat lady sings." She leans in and stage-whispers, "And I'm the fat lady."

"What?"

"What?" She flutters her long lashes again.

"Ooo-kay," I say. Weirdness is part and parcel with Mina. "I have no idea what you're talking about."

"You will soon."

"Popcorn!" Daniel comes back carrying a big bag, and

hands it to Mina. "And settle down, kids, the movie's starting soon."

For a few minutes, Mina and I gossip together, catching up. Apparently Daniel did find and fly her over, just to spend the weekend with me.

The light in the park is dwindling to twilight. But the lights over the stage are on and lending enough light for people to find their seats.

Mina lifts a newspaper and spreads it out as if she can read it. "Have the paparazzi given you any more trouble?" she asks, out of nowhere.

"No. Probably because I stayed inside for two weeks."

"Hmmm," Daniel says. "So I take it you haven't been watching the news?"

"No," I say. I banned all media more recent than a Hitchcock film from my life. No men but Cary Grant and Elvis. I told myself I didn't want to risk seeing someone's horrible opinion about me but really, it's because I can't bear to see another picture of Benedict.

"Really? I think you should read the front page today. It's very interesting." Mina pushes the paper into my lap.

Benedict's face in profile catches my eye, but there's also a picture of the outside of the palace. With the blurred figure of a falling person.

I gasp at the headline: DUKE DEFENESTRATES VISCOUNT'S SON.

My eyes flash over the first paragraph and my mouth falls open. Benedict pushed Chadwick out the window?

"Isn't it epic?" Mina says. "Benedict punched him. They fought, and Chadwick-the-Dick Cawthorne ended up going head first through the window."

"It was an old window," Daniel puts in. "Chad wasn't badly hurt."

Mina takes the paper back and shows me a column below the fold. "See? He fell into a hedge."

"A hedge of thorns. The queen's prized roses, I believe," Daniel says.

The lower half of my jaw sways gently in the breeze. Mina and Daniel reach out together, and lift my chin to a more respectable position.

"By why did he do it?" I croak when I find my voice.

Mina snorts.

Daniel cocks a brow. "You have to ask?"

"He did it for me," I whisper.

"Yes. Not only that; he told the entire government he was a bastard, and renounced the throne," Daniel says.

"No," I gasp.

"Yes." Mina crunches on popcorn, watching us with obvious enjoyment, as if we're the movie she came to see. I would enjoy it more if the plot wasn't my life.

"He can't do that." I grab Daniel's arm. "You have to stop him."

"Frankie, it's done."

"But… why? He can't throw it all away… He's worked so hard!" My voice is rising.

"Shhh," Daniel murmurs, but now people are watching. "In his eyes, he's not throwing anything away. He told me he's gaining something worth any price. Or someone."

Mina sets aside the popcorn and dusts off her hands. "Let me," she says to Daniel, and he nods and sits back in his seat.

"Real talk, girlfriend," Mina says, and turns me to face her. Full frontal—I know she's serious. She'll pull no punches. "Douchey McDouche Face and his family hurt you." Douchey McDouche Face is Chadwick Cawthorne. "And you ran away from society for eight years."

I make a noise of protest and she waves it away. "You make a living moving around and living alone, with no one to talk to but a dog, or cat, or the occasional parrot. You never even leave the houses you stay in, if you can help it."

She's not wrong, but the best defense is a good offense. "Oh, like you can talk, Mina," I scoff. "You told me you once didn't leave your apartment for six months. You would've gone longer if the roof hadn't leaked."

"That's different." Mina waves it off. "I'm different. I'm a mushroom. Or a vampire. A mushroom vampire. I do best in darkness and solitude. As long as I have computers, I have friends."

I start to argue, and she overrides me. "But you, Frankie," she shakes my shoulders lightly, "you weren't meant to hide. You were meant to shine."

Her compliment hits me hard, and I bite back tears.

"You've been hiding, Frankie. And you're too gorgeous and wonderful to hide away. You had more thorns around you than Sleeping Beauty's castle. And then a handsome duke broke you out."

"Technically, Elvis the parrot did," Daniel puts in.

"Whatever." Mina is undeterred. "He broke you out, and put you in the spotlight where you belong. And then you," she shakes my shoulders again, "you returned the favor. You set him free."

"He's been happier than he's been in years," Daniel adds. "Ever. Since I've known him. When he was with you, he smiled. He used to smile only when it was time to audit the War Department. Now, he smiles for no reason."

"Not no reason," Mina corrects Daniel, and looks back at me. "You're the reason."

"You're the reason," Daniel agrees. "It's a fairytale."

"It's a fucking fairytale," Mina repeats. "You even sing with birds, like a Disney princess. It's so cute, it makes me want to puke."

I laugh and wipe my eyes. "You guys are too nice," I whisper.

"No, we're not," Mina says. "But it's for your own good." She winds her arm around me. I think she's trying to hug me, so I reciprocate. She says something else, but it's muffled by our hug.

"Pardon me?" I draw back.

"Don't run away." Her dark brown eyes are deadly serious. Her arms clamp around me tightly.

A mic on stage squeaks. A man has taken the stage, approaching a podium that wasn't there three minutes ago. He's tall, dark, and sinfully hot in a suit.

Benedict.

Now Daniel has an arm linked with mine. He and Mina are hanging on to me as if I'm about to rear and gallop off like a wild horse.

But I don't move. I can't take my eyes off the stage.

Benedict looks a tad thinner. He's the only one wearing a suit to an outdoor movie night. If he could legislate Casual Fridays out of existence, he probably would. I bite my lip. I had planned to introduce him to the concept of leisure wear if we ever moved in together.

"Ladies and Gentlemen," Benedict announces, and the crowd quiets down. "Welcome to the first classic movie night and fireworks in the park. The first of many. Made possible by our Treasury department." He takes a deep breath, and looks straight at me. "But first, we need to thank the woman who made it all possible. She gave me the idea, you see."

My heart seizes. Mina and Daniel let go of my arms.

"Go," my friends urge.

I rise on shaking legs. *It's just theater. It's just an act.* But I don't know what part I'm supposed to play.

All I know is the man I love is on stage, and I might be terrified, but I can't walk away.

The stage creaks a little under my first step. But I gain confidence as I walk. Enough to pull off my headscarf. There's a gasp from the audience but I don't waver. Benedict is waiting for me.

I'm glad Daniel did my hair.

I halt a few feet away, not sure what to do. Benedict steps away from the mic, but when he speaks, his voice carries like he's been theater trained. Or maybe the hillside acoustics are just that good. "Lady Beatrice, have you wept all this while?"

The reply comes to my lips automatically. "Yea, and I will weep a while longer."

"I will not desire that." His gaze is tender.

"You have no reason. I do it freely." My lips part and my eyes flutter. I know what Benedict is going to say next.

He takes his time, swaying carefully forward so we're inches apart. "I do love nothing in the world so well as you: is not that strange."

"Wooohooo, yeah!" Mina shouts from the audience.

I open my mouth but I can't remember my line. Benedict is holding me, and looking at me like I'm the only person in the world, and I'm falling, falling…

And then I remember. "I love you with so much of my heart that none is left to protest." I gasp the words, and cover my mouth so my heart doesn't leap out. The words scare me so much, but I couldn't keep them in any more than I could keep my heart from beating.

And Benedict is right here. His hand on my arm steadies me.

"I will live in thy heart," he draws me close, "die in thy lap," he cups my cheek with his right hand, "and be buried in thy eyes."

"Die in my lap, huh?" I gaze up at him, chest heaving like I've run a mile. I summon a wicked smile "You know, that is a very naughty reference."

"Stay with me, Frankie." His breath caresses my lips. "Be naughty with me."

"Smooch! Smooch! Smooch!" Mina cheers. The audience picks up her chant.

His arms slide around me, and I rise to tiptoe. The crowd bursts into cheers. Our heads slant, and our lips touch right as the first firework pops, and lights up the night.

Deep in a conservatory room masquerading as a jungle, two grey-haired women sit over tea. One is as stout as she is tall, with ruddy cheeks and a no nonsense look about her—Lady Ursaline. The other is Lady Ursaline's oldest and best friend, Lady Drey. Lady Drey is tall and thin, with an African Grey parrot perched on her shoulder.

Both have a stack of digestive biscuits on their plates. Lady Drey is feeding her stack to her parrot, Elvis.

Lady Ursaline sips her tea loudly and smacks her lips. "It was lovely, Tiffy. So sorry you missed it. This country hasn't had a good defenestration since 1866."

"Really?" Lady Drey arches a delicate eyebrow. "I'm surprised you know that."

Lady Ursaline puffs up. "Of course I know it. It was my bloody ancestor who did the defenestrating. Benedict's namesake, actually. The same one who triumphed in the schnitzel eating contest and won the throne." She heaves a sigh that ruffles Elvis' feathers. "My, those were the days. They don't make royals with the stuff anymore. Not until

Benny, and he's, well, he's a bastard." She sounds proud of his illegitimate status.

"He's doing very well at the Ministry of Finance, from what I hear," Lady Drey says. "And using his personal funds to host movie nights at the parks was inspired. I hear they are very popular. In a few years' time, he might have enough goodwill to run for President or Prime Minister."

"Yes, yes, one way or another, that boy will do his duty for the country." Lady Ursaline waves a hand, disrupting Elvis again. "All's well that ends well."

"Don't you mean *Much Ado About Nothing?*" Lady Drey murmurs, smoothing her parrot's feathers.

Lady Ursaline doesn't seem to hear. "But that's not why I called on you, Tiffy."

"Yes, you sounded quite put out on the phone. Do tell, Teddy. I will do all I can to help."

"Well, as you know, the queen's pregnancy is progressing nicely. But there's still a matter of succession, at least until her progeny comes of age."

"Yes, I heard. The Marquis of Dupree is next in line?"

"Yes. Franz. But he is quite unfit. Not at all like his brother Benedict, except, well, Franz is legitimate. I must groom young Franz into someone more presentable. More suited to the throne."

"Ah, yes." Lady Drey nods as she feeds Elvis a cookie. "And what will you do to rehabilitate him?"

"My dear Tiffy," Lady Ursaline pulls a folder out of her oversized purse, "I am so glad you asked."

Lady Drey plucks her spectacles from the table and sets them on the end of her nose, leaning in to study the photographs Lady Ursuline has spread out beside the tea tower.

"There's not a man or woman Franz listens to or respects

in this kingdom." Lady Ursuline plants a finger on the photograph beside a young woman's face. "Except her."

"Who is she?"

"An art student working as a governess. Teaching the children of the Head of the Ministry of Civil Aviation. She's lovely. And wise."

Lady Drey looks up to smile at her oldest and dearest friend. "I see you have a plan, Teddy."

Lady Ursuline chuckles. "Oh, yes." She holds up the photograph of the young woman. "And my plans all revolve around her…"

AUTHOR'S NOTE

Thanks for reading Benedict & Frankie's story!

Special thanks to Aubrey Cara for beta reading, and constant encouragement. Dedicated to everyone who saved my sanity in 2020.

No parrots were harmed in the making of this book.

Dark & Sexy Paranormal romance

The Berserker Saga and Berserker Brides (menage werewolves)

These fierce warriors will stop at nothing to claim their mates.

Draekons (Dragons in Exile) with Lili Zander (menage alien dragons)

Crashed spaceship. Prison planet. Two big, hulking, bronzed aliens who turn into dragons. The best part? The dragons insist I'm their mate.

Bad Boy Alphas with Renee Rose (bad boy werewolves)

Never ever date a werewolf.

Tsenturion Masters with Golden Angel

Who knew my e-reader was a portal to another galaxy? Now I'm stuck with a fierce alien commander who wants to claim me as his own.

ABOUT LEE SAVINO

Lee Savino has plans to take over the world, but most days can't find her keys or her phone, so she just stays home and writes smexy (smart + sexy) romance. She loves chocolate, lives in yoga pants, and looks great in hats.

For tons of crazy fun, join her Goddess Group on Facebook or visit www.leesavino.com to sign up for her mailing list and get a free book.

Website: www.leesavino.com

www.ingramcontent.com/pod-product-compliance
Lightning Source LLC
Chambersburg PA
CBHW050324110726
47899CB00007B/2362